ANNE BOLEYN'S GHOST

Anne Boleyn's Ghost by Liam Archer

Copyright © 2013 Liam Archer

All rights reserved. No part of this publication may be reproduced, stored in a retrieval system, or transmitted, in any form or by any means, electronic, mechanical, photocopying, recording, or otherwise, unless permitted by the UK Copyright, Designs and Patents Act 1988, without the prior written permission of the publisher.

ISBN 978-1494736484

Photography by Liam Archer

First Edition

Contents

	Introduction	I
I	The Visit to Hever Castle	3
II	In the Darkroom	20
III	The Photographs	23
IV	The Difference between the Camera and the Eye	30
V	Anne's Story	32
VI	How it Began	35
VII	The Break from Rome	4I
VIII	The Coronation	43
IX	Elizabeth Arrives	47
X	The King's Will	5I
XI	Untimely Mishap	53
XII	Devising a Plan	56
XIII	Losing her Freedom	62
XIV	The Accused are Heard	67
XV	Final Days	74
	Sightings of Anne's Ghost	83

Introduction

I

It was midsummer 2009, when I went with family and friends to visit Hever Castle on the five hundredth anniversary of King Henry the Eighth's Accession to the Throne. In the past, I visited Hever Castle on several occasions, and I have many cherished memories of the castle. Hever Castle was by no means the only castle I visited with family on more than one occasion. By the time I was ten years old I had been to so many castles, I couldn't possibly count them all – such as Tintagel Castle in Cornwall; Cardiff Castle in Wales; Windsor Castle; and the infamous Tower of London, to name a few.

Shortly after my thirteenth birthday I discovered *photography*. Winter was coming to a close, and the days were growing increasingly warmer. One sunny day I came across a disposable camera lying vacantly on top of a cabinet at home. I picked it up, looked at the dial on top, and noticed it had a full roll of film. So without further ado I took the camera downstairs, went into the front garden, and looked for something to photograph.

I spotted a small group of newly emerged daffodils, all bunched together and thriving in the warmth, while surrounding tall trees broke up and softened the sun's golden rays. I took a few steps towards them, peered through the viewfinder, and started to take pictures. As I clicked happily away I found myself searching for dramatic angles: my chin grazed the grass; the camera twisted and turned one way, then the other; all until my little box became silent. And with the glorious day ahead of me, I took the camera back inside, where I immediately forgot about it, and spent the rest of the day doing more important things, *like* skateboarding.

Nevertheless that tiny fragment of my day would prove to be much more significant in my life than I first gave it credit for, and was a subtle sign of a gift and love I would come to appreciate in the years that soon followed.

Halfway through high school I took my first ever photography course. It combined the practical side of shooting and camera operation, with film development and printing. I passed the course with an outstanding grade, and thoroughly impressed my teacher, as well as many of my classmates, with my photographs.

Later that year I was given my first SLR camera for my sixteenth birthday. It opened up a whole new world as I soon began to discover life through the lens. There seemed to be a kind of magic about photography, ingrained within its wizardry. A part of its magic seemed to be in the sheer mystery of the *unknown* – with this 'unknown' having two parts: firstly, the fairly long period of time between taking a photograph and seeing the final result (as is the case with a traditional film camera); secondly, the difference between observing what you intend to capture, and how that will transpose on to film (the final result).

It wasn't long until digital cameras became popular, and I bought a compact digital camera, as I followed the trend. It became seldom that I used my SLR after that: the convenience and practicality of digital technology was a big advantage, and one that was not easy to overlook, even if my older SLR was inherently a better camera. I also enjoyed seeing my photographs immediately after they were taken – something that took away some of the mystery from the process, but in turn had made photography less expensive and more accessible – and I liked being able to take a camera with me virtually everywhere I went. Ultimately my SLR began to gather some dust.

Despite my likeness of digital technology I didn't go ahead and buy a digital *SLR* camera. This was mainly because I already owned a perfectly good SLR, and had had great results from it for years. I enjoyed doing photography as a hobby, and compact digital cameras were perfect for someone like me: an enthusiast and someone that never liked to miss a shot.

Chapter I

The Visit to Hever Castle

Shortly before our family trip to Hever Castle I accompanied my mum on one bright Saturday afternoon as we went to the local Garden Centre. Having made a habit of bringing a camera with me on pretty much every outing, I had brought along my fairly new digital camera for the short trip.

When we returned home later that day I pressed my coat pocket, expecting to feel the chunky candy-bar shaped camera inside; but it wasn't there. Somehow it had managed to slide out of my pocket at some point during the day, and it wasn't about to grow a small pair of legs and find its way back to its rightful owner. It was lost.

Our visit to Hever Castle was less than two weeks away, and the only camera I could bring now was my older, heavier, SLR camera. The large size of the camera, and the general inconvenience of having to buy film, made the camera more bothersome to bring on long outings than a compact; and it had been more than two years since I had used my SLR for anything more than taking a few photos in town. However, left with no other choice (short of going without a camera at all) I went in search for the right batteries as the day to visit the castle neared. I tried not to be too disappointed about losing my nifty compact. Actually I felt rather excited that I would *have* to bring my bulkier SLR along, which had rarely seen the light of day for years, and had seemed all but destined to antiquity.

I didn't think much about it at the time; I was just glad I was going to be able to take some photos when I got there.

Hever Castle

The History of Hever Castle

Hever Castle was built shortly after the Norman Conquest when the land on which the castle was eventually built was given to a Norman noble, called Walter de Hevere. The oldest part of Hever Castle dates back to the late thirteenth century when Walter's grandson, William, converted the original farmhouse into a manor and castle, consisting of a huge gatehouse, a wooden drawbridge, and a motte and walled bailey. In 1459 the Lord Mayor of London, Sir Geoffrey Bullen (later changed to 'Boleyn') became the proud owner of the castle. Three years later the castle underwent a period of renovation that transformed the imposing defensive structure into a mysterious home suitable for raising a family. The castle was then inherited by Geoffrey's son William, who, in 1505, passed ownership on to his son, Thomas, shortly before he died. When Thomas Boleyn married Elizabeth Howard, Hever Castle became the mysterious home for him, his wife and three newborn children: *Anne, Mary* and *George*.

A few years later Thomas Boleyn extended the castle by adding the *Long Gallery*. In 1538 Thomas died and his brother gained ownership of the castle; though it was soon seized the following year by King Henry the Eighth. In 1540 Henry gave the castle to his fourth wife, Anne of Cleves, as a part of their divorce settlement. From 1557 onwards the castle was owned by these three families: the Waldegraves, the Meade Waldos, and the Astors. In 1903 William Waldorf Astor purchased and invested in Hever Castle by extending the grounds with a mock Tudor village, gardens, and a lake; as well as numerous Italian sculptures of his that gave the grounds a distinctive theme and a romantic *twist*. Today the castle is open to the public, having long since out-lived its day as a home for nobility, royalty and commoners alike for nearly eight hundred years.

*

On July 25th, 2009 my mother, brother, his partner and I arrived in Kent by train. It was shortly after two o'clock when we stepped off on to the narrow and empty platform. As soon as a taxi pulled up we got inside and went along Kent's narrow and winding roads, accompanied by our chatty driver, towards Hever Castle. Peering out the window, light grey clouds filled the sky, and it looked bound to rain at any moment; but, oddly enough, on arriving at our destination, and the foliage overhead gradually subsiding, the sun shone warmly through.

We soon bought our tickets, and with every step the castle's majestic walls slowly began to emerge in the valley. The first thing I had to do was buy some film for my camera; and so off we went to Hever's Gift Shop.

After waiting ten minutes or so in the long queue, which appeared to have been caused by a woman who was arguing with the cashier, because her card wasn't being read by the machine, I bought two rolls of film, loaded one of them into my camera and met up with the others, who had made good use of the time and were now carrying several bags full of souvenirs.

Next, we all headed to the café, situated near the lake, for lunch. The sunshine was short lived: rain began to fall lightly, and thick grey clouds once again blanketed the sky. As we made our way towards the café I began to take photos of the gardens and sculptures – taking care not to get my camera wet, and routinely wiping the lens with the sleeve of my shirt at each tiny spec of rain that fell upon it.

We stopped by the Loggia Fountain, where a reenactment of a Tudor scene was taking place: the men and women were all dressed in colourful clothing and sitting around a table playing a game of cards in the portico. A handful of rowboats were out on the lake, and almost everybody had their umbrellas open, though the rain was *especially* light. I took some photos of the fountain – its cherubs pouring and whistling water forth – and the lake, before carrying on with the others to the café.

Once there we sat outside in the drizzle while we had some tea and cake. Fifteen minutes or so later we left our table and started walking back towards the castle, all of us now much looking forward to seeing its quirky old rooms; and for one hour almost traveling back in time to the sixteenth century.

I took a few more photographs of a pair of empty rowboats that drifted idly under a willow tree in shallow water, and some of the castle as we arrived outside its enchanted walls. The clouds had almost entirely vanished since our short walk back from the cafe, revealing a baby-blue sky; and occasional blustery gusts of wind gave this seemingly picturesque view a touch of *electricity*. Families were making their way over the old wooden drawbridge, and enjoying the sun outside the castle's walls, when my first roll of film began to wind itself up inside my camera of its own accord, and I sat on a nearby bench as I removed it and loaded a second roll of film in its place.

And with my camera ready to go, I was eager to capture the castle *it-*

self.

We passed over the drawbridge, through the grand gatehouse arch and into the small enclosed courtyard. Wind was rendered non-existent by the castle's high encompassing walls, and the blue sky floated airily above the courtyard as the sun's inviting light lit up the Tudor manor.

The Drawbridge, Hever Castle

I approached the front-door, reached for the handle and pulled, but the door would not open. We glanced at the timetable, and, checking the time, realized we had arrived one minute late – we had arrived at 4:01, and the doors were closed at 4:00.

A glum felling overcame us all. Not knowing what to do, we looked at each other a shade disheartened, almost sure we would have to head back home without going inside the castle.

But having *just* missed the closing time, we endeavored to enter. The door behind us seemed to be a part of the gatehouse, and was wide open with an *exit* sign beside it. So without further delay, we all went inside and climbed the stone spiral staircase, hoping to find someone who could help us once we had reached the first floor.

Mildly surprising members of staff as we entered the dimly lit room, we asked if we could be let in, having been a minute late, and were told to knock on the front-door and ask for a certain member of staff, who would let us in.

Having gone back down the same spiral staircase, with its sharp twist, we approached the front-door once again, hoping, this time, we would contrive to enter. The courtyard was now completely empty, and had become a pale-grey hue from the prevailing cloud cover (which had reappeared as quickly as it went, as if time itself was jumping in leaps and bounds). And there we stood, in the grand and quiet courtyard, wondering who would go up and knock on the castle's ancient front-door.

The Tudor Manor, Hever Castle

Complete silence fell upon us, caused by an underlying and inexplicable apprehensiveness of this one simple task. It was almost as if a veil had been lifted from the castle; the walls appeared oddly larger than they were only minutes before; and it felt like we had suddenly found ourselves anxious guests, patiently waiting to be let into a home of *royalty* ...

My mother went up and knocked on the door with four consecutive timely knocks that echoed eerily in the empty courtyard. After a minute or so the dark oak door slowly opened, revealing a petite young woman behind it.

'We were told to ask for *Anne*?' And just like saying the magic words, we were soon crossing the threshold into the castle.

As I approached the doorway I couldn't help but notice how dark it seemed inside. Tilting my head as I entered to avoid hitting the door's frame, we were all now happily inside; and it appeared that we were the only visitors left inside the castle. I turned towards the part of the room that was better lit by the windows, as my eyes adjusted to the room's thin light. Looking around to see if anybody apart from ourselves was inside the castle, the only thing that indicated we weren't alone was the faint creaking of floorboards as people shuffled along on the floor directly above.

The door closed behind us; the latch fell quietly into place. I looked back, unaware that the lady who had let us in was still standing nearby; and by the time I had turned round again, the others had moved through the ground floor so quickly, they were now almost completely out of sight; their footsteps hadn't made a sound. 'Why are they in such a rush?' I thought. As I watched them from where I stood, rooted, I thought about catching up with them, so I wouldn't fall behind; but then I was determined to take my time, and felt a little perplexed as to their quickness: so I decided I would have a little look round, and would catch up with the others once I had.

It was a fairly large room, and the windows were all to one. Nothing in particular caught my eye, so I didn't dawdle. I was now completely alone (from what I could see, anyway), and felt quite at home strolling along, as I got a feel for what it might have been like to have actually lived here. Never, not during one of the several times I had been inside this castle, had I once walked through these rooms, so steeped in history, by myself. And for the very first time I began to see Hever Castle, not as a museum containing relics of an age that had long since past, but as a *home*.

I turned a corner that led into the living-room, at the centre of which was a grand fireplace; and a little further on, as I approached the staircase, the room was almost asking me to capture it, being free from the daily brushes of tourists and workers. I looked back towards the staircase, to see if the others, and caught a brief glimpse of someone as they turned a corner up the short flight of stairs. Realizing I wasn't too far behind, I began to get my camera ready.

As I placed my camera bag on the floor, I saw the metal-base of the lamp next to me was *shifting* subtly, from side to side, and appeared to vibrate like strings on a musical instrument. I didn't have my glasses with me, so I wasn't able to trust my eyes entirely, even though the lamp was within an arm's reach to my right and close enough for me to discern; and I resumed getting my camera ready, thinking: 'That's a *bit* strange…'

I wanted to photograph the focal points of the room, being the fireplace, furniture, and paintings on the walls. I switched my camera on, set it to *auto*, peered through the viewfinder, and got the room into frame. I pressed the shutter release halfway down, when the flash flipped up as I took the first shot: the flash pulsing continuously like a strobe as the room seemed to starve itself of light; and, outside the corner of my eye, *shadowy* uneven light was falling throughout the room, as if invisible clouds lurked within.

Immediately after the first shot I turned my camera ninety degrees clockwise and took a second; this time, however, my flash did not go off: the room hadn't darkened. With two photographs taken, I felt content with what I had captured, as there wasn't much else to see of this room. I placed my camera back in its black-leather bag; and as I stood up and turned to face the staircase, ready to leave, I saw a very faint *elongated ray* of white light moving in a slow, subtle, *snake-like* fashion through mid-air towards the stairs, where it had quickly faded into thin air.

Anne Boleyn's Bedchamber, Hever Castle

Having ascended the staircase, I arrived on the first floor and walked directly into the bedchamber that had belonged to Anne Boleyn, where I was pleased to find the others contently looking round and hadn't gone on too far ahead without me. The original furniture and artwork, as well as the smallness of such a private space, gave the room an intimate and rather *heavy* feel.

After ten minutes, we were all just about to move on to the next room, when I asked my fellow travelers to bear in mind I was taking photographs inside the castle, and wanted to capture the rooms unobstructed and as they were. They all seemed fine with that; and with this request being taken onboard by them, I was capturing the upstairs rooms in the same manner as I had done in the living-room on the ground floor: empty apart from the furnishings.

Once again I got my camera out and looked around for the focal points of the room; this time it was a portrait of Anne Boleyn, the bed-head, and the bay window. I peered through the viewfinder and got the room into frame, and took the first of three shots. Each time I released the shutter my body became statue-like, as if I was not only freezing time through my photographs, but as if I myself had been frozen in time in the process. Having taken three shots, the only difference this time was how well lit the room was by the bay window, so my camera's flash hadn't gone off. As we walked out I placed my hand on the intricate wooden bed-head as I went, *for* good luck.

The next room housed several charming sixteenth century objects. Numerous items belonged to Anne Boleyn, and almost everything appeared encased in glass showcases. This room was dimly lit and busy with visitors, so I kept my camera stowed away. A minute or two had passed, and I was finding it difficult to see well in the darkness, when something was pointed out to me; it was a small and brightly coloured blue prayer book that was given to Anne Boleyn shortly before she was executed at the Tower of London, bearing the inscription: *Remember me when you do pray that hope doth lead from day to day*. Because the room was so dark, it made the objects, and especially the little prayer book my eyes were fixed on, all the more entrancing. After spending a brief period of time in here, we swiftly carried on to the next room.

The room that followed was the bedchamber that had belonged to Anne Boleyn's brother, George. It was yet another fairly small room, which reminded me of a cabin on an old ship; his saber and portrait displayed side by side just added to the adventurous feel of the room. It was bright and pleasant to be in; but time was short and we wanted to see as much of the castle as we could before close, so we continued on.

Further along, I saw a small prayer room tucked away at the far end of the hall. Adorned with guilding, a soft luminous light shone out of it. I wondered why the light appeared so fogged, and went to take a closer look. Peering in, I saw a faint but very apparent mist suspended in mid-air in the centre of the room.
'*Humidity, perhaps* ...' I thought, as I walked slowly away.
In the narrow and wonky hallway, I stopped by a portrait of Anne Boleyn's only daughter, Elizabeth, depicting her as the Queen of England. The painting echoed what I had seen, just a short while before, on the base of the lamp downstairs; but this time it was much more intense (or at least appeared so, standing so close to it in the narrow hallway); so much so that the painting looked as if it was made, not of canvas, but of hundreds of finely painted moths that had suddenly awoken, and were stirring energetically within the frame. I looked away as my eyes seemed to fail me, and continued walking down the hallway as if a strong current had suddenly uprooted me.

The next room we entered was the bedchamber that was likely home to Henry the Eighth, when he had stayed at the castle. The room certainly would've been fit for a king, with its large fireplace, intricate carvings, and stately bed. I was yearning to photograph a room that was once inhabited by England's best known King.
After taking the shot, a member of staff stopped outside the room, and said from the hallway: 'No cameras –'
For a second or more I didn't know what to say, having been somewhat startled by his voice. 'But it is such a *beautiful* room ...' I replied earnestly, voicing the first thing that came to mind. Hoping I wasn't in too much trouble. I stared at him: a soft blur gazing back at me from the length of the hallway; and before I could say anything more, he was gone. From then on I was determined not to take anymore photographs inside the castle, and possibly risk losing my film, or, perhaps, my only camera.
After climbing a small staircase, we passed through another narrow hallway comprised of some very eerie children's bedrooms, and entered the *Long Gallery*. This room was visually the most spectacular out of all the rooms I had been in. As soon as I stepped inside I became awestruck

by the ornate ceiling, which looked as if it had been crafted by no less than ten of the world's most scrupulous artisans.

I stopped halfway across the Gallery as I was met by a series of models of Henry the Eighth and his six wives. I remembered them from when I had visited the castle some ten years before, and was pleased to see they were still here, adding to the theatrics of the space. For some reason the model of Anne Boleyn stood out visibly from the other models. I stood for awhile and gazed at it; the eyes appeared uncannily more life-like than the others; and it drew all of my attention towards it as I was engaged by *unseemly dark pearls that hovered below the brow*. I looked briefly at the models of Anne of Cleves and Jane Seymore, trying to see something similar in them; but they all lacked that *strange ghostly veil*.

When I arrived at the end of the Long Gallery, I raised my eyes to the ceiling once again and found myself spellbound by *its mystique*, and *its complexity* ... I had to take *one last shot*.

I hesitated, listening carefully for the pitter-patter of people moving about the halls: there were so few people still inside the castle. When nothing seemed to be louder than a heartbeat, I quickly removed my camera from its bag, inclined it towards the ceiling, and ... *click* –

The final room we entered was the room we had actually entered first: when we went the spiral staircase of the gatehouse seeking assistance from staff. This room was part of the castle's defenses, displaying tools that would have been used to torture enemies of the King – or Queen, most likely, while Anne lived her later years at the castle. After a brief look at what was on display, which included a murder-hole and several tools that looked more in-keeping with masonry, than objects that were used on the flesh and bones of man, we headed back down the steep spiral staircase, exited the gatehouse, and in the courtyard were met by a dreary grey *English* sky.

The Courtyard, Hever Castle

I was a little more than halfway through my second roll of film, and the courtyard with its striking arch was the perfect place to take a few more photographs, now that I was out of the castle and could safely use my camera again.

As we began to make our way out, I sought to finish my second roll of film by capturing the castle's grounds; and after a few more shots just outside the ticket stands of the church and pub close by, the *hum* of film reeling inside my camera indicated its completion, and I stowed my camera safely away, knowing I would see the developed photographs in just a few weeks' time.

* * *

Outside the main entrance to Hever Castle, across the road from the ticket stands, is the *King Henry VIII pub*. We were all hungry; and with it being a convenient place to stop and eat, we decided to go there for dinner.

Seated at our table, I was looking over the *Specials* Menu, when the waitress stopped by us and said there was a long wait, – it being Sunday – because the pub was exceptionally busy. With no other pub or restaurant nearby, we decided to stay put and ordered a few snacks from the bar to pass the time.

Twenty minutes had gone by, and I was quietly sipping my drink and peering out a back-door window on to the patio, where people were dining comfortably under glowing gas-heaters, when Mum asked if I was feeling alright. Having been a bit surprised by this question, I said I was feeling alright. Then she said I looked rather pale, which was quickly reiterated by both my brother and his partner. Now that they had asked, I suddenly realized how unwell I felt, but thought I just needed some food, having not eaten much all day; little did I know of my ghostly encounter less than an hour before within Hever Castle.

We were all looking forward to having our meals, when, quite unexpectedly, an argument rang out from the kitchen. Everybody gradually fell silent as the chatter in the pub was drowned out by the ensuing shouts. After it had quieted down, the waitress walked out of the kitchen and announced to everyone that the chef would not cook anymore meals, and that there was no other chef on site. Everyone meekly resumed with their Sunday roasts, and could hardly return to the buzzing tone that had filled the pub only minutes before; and we were frustrated for having waited on the up-side of half an hour already, and asked the waitress for an explanation about the sudden upset.

THE VISIT TO HEVER CASTLE

After a sincere apology and some insight, we put on our coats and began to make our way out of the pub; and as we made for the door, the chef walked out of the kitchen and was in view of all the unsettled customers: he didn't say anything, but looked disgruntled and red-faced. We had to find a different restaurant to dine at; and on attempting to arrange a taxi to take us to one, the soonest available taxi was nearly a two hour wait. Things weren't running quite as smoothly as we had hoped. We asked the waitress where the nearest restaurant was, and she gave us some directions that would lead us to one, being about a thirty minute walk. With no alternative, we set off along the narrow country roads, taking the upmost care to listen out for approaching cars as it was difficult to see with the roads' numerous bends and blind spots.

Eventually, after one or two missed turns, we had all safely arrived at *The Greyhound Bed & Breakfast*. It was a delightful place to end up after all the trouble; it had a pleasant interior, a hearty menu, and a warm cosy ambiance. Having treated myself to a steak, I was starving, so as soon as it had arrived I took a large bite and accidentally ate a heap of peppercorns hidden under the thick cream sauce. I immediately began to feel even more unwell, and now my palely hue turned a shade green as I did my best to enjoy the meal, in spite of it.

When dinner finally came to a close, we all made our way back to the train station, and then home.

Chapter II

In the Darkroom

Three months had gone by. It was the middle of October, and the day at Hever Castle was firmly in the past and had been all but off my mind. Then, remembering I still had my film to develop, I took the two canisters to a local shop to have them turned into prints. One week later they would be ready for me to pick up. I felt excited when I recalled how many photos I had taken inside the castle, and I was interested to see how they had all turned out.

It was a sunny, blustery October day and the town was bustling with life. I almost couldn't wait to see the photographs after all this time, having practically forgotten about them. Once I had paid for them, I walked over to a nearby bench and thought about opening them then and there; but when I realized how thick the envelopes were, and that this was no place to view them quietly, or free from wind, I decided to take them home where I could view them in some solitude.

As soon as I got back, I went straight into the living-room, sat down on the sofa, and started going through the two large envelopes. The first set contained the pictures of Hever's gardens and lake. After taking a brief look at that set, I was fairly curious to see the ones I had taken *inside* the castle.

At first, everything appeared to be what I was expecting: an image of the castle from afar, some nice clear shots of the courtyard, and a striking shot of the gatehouse arch. But as I looked at the very first photograph I had taken inside Hever Castle, I knew I had captured something I couldn't quite put my finger on...

I gazed steadfastly at the image, trying my hardest to decipher its light; and for a few, impossibly long minutes I was none the wiser as to what on earth I was looking at. As my brain scrambled in the midst of an image not a lifetime's worth of photographic experience could have prepared me for – let alone five years' – all of a sudden a triumphant rush of excitement surged inside me, as something *finally* stood out.

There, in plain sight, was a woman's ghostly hand, frozen in the far left of the frame. *How could this be?* I remembered being there like it was yesterday: *nobody* was in that room with me when I took that photograph. But something told me, from the very first second I had set my eyes upon it, that this was no ordinary woman's hand, because the hand wasn't the only *strange* thing that had appeared in the photograph.

The light emitted from both of the lamps now appeared stretched and curved in what seemed to be the direction of the hand; a large streak of white light lay at the top right of the frame, bearing an unmistakable resemblance to the *snake-like* ray I had seen undulating its way toward the staircase; and blue swirly slivers of light hung enigmatically below the lamp and portrait in the distance. This was no ordinary photograph: this was a photograph of *a Ghost*.

I brought the photograph over to my mum, who was in the kitchen, and showed her what I could see in it. 'Remember the photos I took inside Hever Castle –?' I said, holding it up '– there's a ghost in it: a *hand*. Look!'

At that point she took the photograph from me and gazed fixedly at it. She appeared flummoxed by it, and I had to point out the Ghost as she struggled, as I did, to ascertain the image before her. Not surprisingly, everyone who saw my ghost photographs over the next few weeks either couldn't believe their eyes, or were simply unwilling to, in an age when Hollywood visuals has done every photographic trick in the book (though, I must admit, one or two people really were gobsmacked by them, and seemed to believe me, which was reassuring). I was a little surprised by this; but it didn't bother me too much. I was confident in my own judgment, and nothing could change that. I also thought about how I would've reacted if somebody I knew claimed to have photographed a Ghost, and I'm sure I would have been just as sceptical.

I still had the whole set to go through, and many more photographs that I had taken inside the castle I hadn't yet seen. With this thought, I demanded to have the picture back from my mother, who, looking over her spectacles, was holding it no more than an inch in front of her, and had been staring intensely at it for what must have been an ice age.

Having retrieved it from her grasp, I went back into the living-room so I could explore the rest of the photographs. I looked for more signs of ghosts specifically, like the apparent hand in the first picture, wondering if the other photographs had something similar in them that could be as easily distinguished. And to my surprise, I wasn't disappointed. The bedhead that belonged to Anne Boleyn was almost entirely unrecognizable; and the portrait of Anne Boleyn appeared to have two heads, side by side … other portraits looked like they had melted out of their frames … and a strange fuzziness pervaded almost every photograph taken inside the castle. I held the negatives up to an overhead light and inspected the ones of the castle's rooms: surely enough, they looked no different to the pictures strewn out in front of me.

Hours passed. And when I had finally grown tired and felt like I had taken it all in, everything seemed to point in only one direction: *It was Anne Boleyn's Ghost.*

Chapter III

The Photographs

Having had the very rare opportunity to photograph within Hever Castle's historic walls, I had captured its spaces with the upmost care and diligence. But despite all that, what my camera saw that day, and what I had *actually* seen, were worlds apart.

Now, take a look at the photographs taken inside Hever Castle. These are the original photographs; and besides some cropping and enlarging to show significant parts of the images, they have not been altered or manipulated in any way. They were all taken with my Canon Rebel Ti 35mm SLR film camera with a 28-90mm lens, on the automatic setting. *Note: only the photographs that appear to have Anne Boleyn's Ghost in them are being shown in this book.*

ANNE BOLEYN'S GHOST

This is the first photograph I took inside Hever Castle:

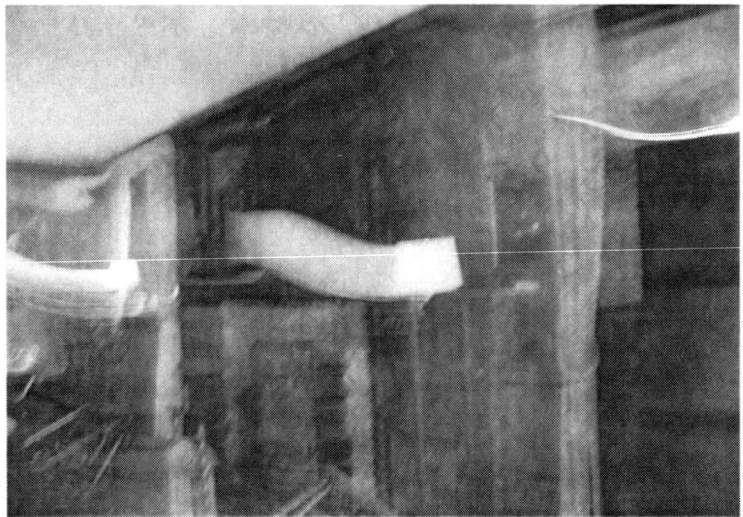

THE PHOTOGRAPHS

To the far left of the frame, a little more than halfway up, is a distinctive hand with an unmistakably feminine appearance. Whoever she is, she seems to be pointing at the wall, and perhaps the fireplace in the middle of the room. Does this ghostly hand belong to Anne Boleyn? How is it possible that someone who died nearly five hundred years ago can appear on film in the twenty-first century?

The lamp light to either side of the fireplace appears to have been pulled, or 'stretched', as if by magnetism, towards the Ghost. Oddly enough, this would explain why my cameras flash activated during the first shot, and not the one taken immediately after, where the lamp light appears to have been significantly less affected and no apparent Ghost can be seen. The blue streaks of light below the lamp at the far end of the room have no visible light source; and the white streak to the top right of the nearest lamp also has no light source, but is similar in shape to the smaller slivers of blue light in the distance. Are these random anomalies that accompany apparitions? Or could they hold greater significance?

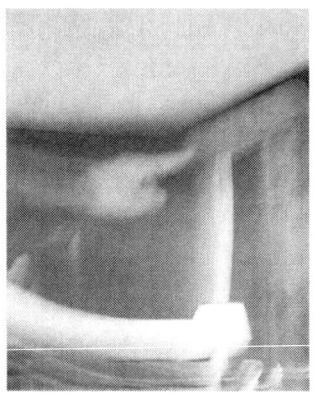

If you look closely, the most remarkable thing about the photograph (apart from the fact that there is a ghost in it) is that part of her dress can be seen clearly; and astonishingly, we can see its form, creases, and, most impressively, its *colour: a dark blue*. The hand is so well defined that individual fingers can be made out; and the one that is pointing curves significantly upwards at its tip.

Anne Boleyn had spent much of her fairly short life at Hever Castle. Is her Ghost haunting the castle today? And if she is, why has she sent us this image of her? Could there be something behind that wall that has been lost for nearly five hundred years ...

THE PHOTOGRAPHS

The next photo is of Anne Boleyn's bedchamber:

Of the three photographs taken in this room, two show strong signs of ghostly phenomena. However, only one shows signs of Anne Boleyn's Ghost, shown above. The photograph that doesn't is backlit and is shown at the beginning of the book (Anne Boleyn's Bedchamber, Hever Castle).

In this frame there is Anne's bed-head, a small side-table, and a portrait of Anne Boleyn. Where her portrait is, two faces can be seen next to each other. This is highly unusual as this distinct splitting of the image has occurred *only* around the portrait. If this had been caused by camera-shake there would be a uniform distortion and splitting of the image. You would expect to see, not only two distinct faces, side by side, as is the case with the portrait; but also two tables, two plants, and two bed-heads. And take a look at the adjacent blank picture hanging on the wall. Why would there be a blank picture hanging on a wall in a regularly visited place, like Hever Castle? Well, that's because it is not blank, but inscribed with some history on Anne Boleyn, if I recall correctly. For some bizarre reason this light never made it into my camera's lens; and when considering that this photograph was taken with a good camera, a fast shutter, no movement, and in a well lit room, it makes this outcome all the harder to explain logically.

THE PHOTOGRAPHS

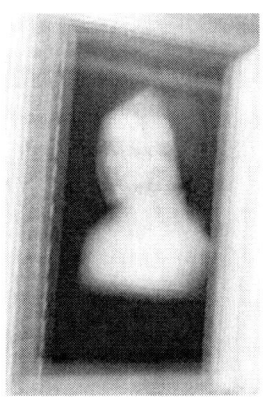

Is this Anne Boleyn's Ghost showing herself in this painting of her? If it was indeed *her* Ghost that had appeared, just a short while before, in the first image – then perhaps she felt that that was the day *Anne Boleyn's Ghost* would reveal herself to the lens, by appearing once more, only this time showing who she really *is*.

Chapter IV

The Difference between the Camera and the Eye

Why couldn't I see what my camera could at Hever Castle, that day in 2009? Apart from the fact that I do not have perfect vision, it might be explained by what capacity the human eye has when observing a scene, compared to a sophisticated camera.

The cameras you and I are familiar with allow light to hit a light-sensitive, chemical-based surface that it then imprints the light on to, and can be physically held as a tangible object. Digital cameras are slightly different as they use sensitive sensors and rely on computer chips to determine the colour and resolution of the image. This capacity to record light accurately is what makes photography so powerful; and it is this that has caused photography to become a worldwide phenomenon, as people now capture and share their images of the world around them, either digitally over the internet, or traditionally with prints and a few interested eyes. However, as lenses have become larger and more complex, computers have been built to assist camera operation, and shutter speeds have become mindboggling fast on consumer models, modern cameras can also see things our eyes cannot.

The human eye is very complex and works much differently to how a camera works. For the human eye, light continually floods in until we blink or close the eyelid, which acts a bit like a camera's shutter. The brain essentially records the light that passes through our eyes organically; and much is still unknown about how the human eye works, while cameras are better understood, because we can study all their various components in great detail, and because we created them.

Cameras, as well as video cameras, are defined in part by what is technically known as frames per second (FPS). This is the speed at which a single image has been captured. For video cameras it's when a single image is immediately followed by another, combining them, and the speed at which it is happening – it's a bit like a flick-book: if each page of the book represents a frame, the faster you flick through the pages, the faster the illustration appears to move, and as if it was *actually* moving.

Modern cameras, and the camera I was using at Hever Castle that day, are capable of seeing greater detail than what you or I are capable of seeing; and the level of detail between them can be, quite literally, universes apart. If you have ever seen a video of a real bullet moving in slow motion, it is not because you or I are capable of seeing a bullet move at walking pace – it's because of *high speed imaging*. The cameras that are used to do this generally capture at speeds that are 1/1000 FPS (that's one thousandth of a second) or faster. The fastest cameras in the world today are used for scientific research, and are capable of capturing light anywhere between two hundred million and one trillion frames per second. The camera I had with me at Hever Castle that day has a maximum of 1/2000 FPS; and although it is not to be compared with the cameras just mentioned it is, however, far superior to my eye when capturing and *recording* a scene in milliseconds.

That is not to say how the eye works is innately inferior to how a camera works – as many cameras are quite basic instruments – so much as cameras are a tool to expand upon our own sight. But without the technological advancements in photography over the past two centuries, many myths would not have been settled, and our knowledge of the universe would be a fraction of what it is today.

For instance in May, 1952 photography was fundamental in identifying the structure of DNA, when Raymond Gosling took a photograph using X-ray diffraction that revealed the double helix.

In 1872 Eadweard Muybridge dispelled the myth as to whether all four feet of a horse came off the ground at the same time when trotting; proving by his photographic sequence that indeed all four feet left the ground together.

And Harold Edgerton, a pioneer in electrical engineering and professor at MIT, shed light on the power of matter, showing us the first ever image of a bullet in mid-flight; the process of a nuclear explosion; and what lay at the depths of our oceans as well as what travels through our skies.

Without photography, we wouldn't have a window into our past or know what our planet looks like from outer space; nor would we be able to observe galaxies or planets where man could never step; the effects of black holes; and some of the most fascinating objects known to science.

Chapter V

Anne's Story

Anne Boleyn was born at the beginning of the sixteenth century at either Blickling Hall or Hever Castle, and was the daughter of a Knight. Her father was Sir Thomas Boleyn, 1st Earl of Wiltshire and Ormond; and her mother was Elizabeth Howard, Countess of Wiltshire. She had two siblings, called Mary and George. Anne Boleyn was highly educated and had studied in both France and the Netherlands. She was brought up on traditional Latin writings, and in her later years studied evangelical texts that she obtained in French, as it was a crime to be seen reading anything other than orthodox scriptures. She was of medium height, and was as beautiful in her looks as in dress. She had brown eyes and dark brown or (some say) black hair, and a long slender neck. Anne Boleyn was the Queen of England for three years, during one of the most turbulent periods in England's history.

Anne Boleyn

She had lived much of her life in France in the company of Queen Claude, wife of Francis the First, and the Duchess of Alencon, as a maid of honour, where she learned her sense of dress. As a result, she could speak French eloquently and with great ease. She sang, danced, and was a learned musician.

Anne Boleyn has been branded a witch by some, mainly because of a rumoured deformity on her right hand, thought to have been a sixth finger. However, her coffin was exhumed in the mid to late nineteenth century when the chapel in which she was buried had undergone restoration work: her skeleton was examined at the time, and it showed no signs of any deformity on it; although many of her bones were found out of place, because her corpse was unceremoniously placed into her coffin (which was actually a small arrow chest) after she was executed. And then of course there is the simple truth that it would have been highly questionable for the King to have been seen courting a woman who had anything about her appearance that might have been considered unusual, or unpleasant on the eye; and certainly not someone who might have been thought to be ... *a witch ...*

As a commoner, Anne Boleyn was not known by the public until her position in society was being elevated by King Henry the Eighth. She was not born into royalty, but knew it was possible for a woman of less privileged origin to achieve such status. When Henry began falling in love with her, he was married to Catherine of Aragon, and had been for almost twenty years. Catherine was a Spanish princess who had been betrothed to Henry's older brother, Arthur; but after his untimely death, Henry was next in line to marry her. During their marriage she gave birth to one son, whose life ended prematurely – causing Henry's dream of patriarchal rule to shatter – and one daughter ... one measly daughter called Mary. From that point on Henry spent the rest of his life trying to restore his fractured dream.

Determined to have Anne Boleyn as his lawful wife, Henry broke away from the Roman Catholic Church to secure the legitimacy of their marriage. The lengths he went to be married to Anne Boleyn were great, and his own ego as being one of the most powerful men in Christendom was the motivating force behind it all.

Chapter VI

How it Began

At the beginning of 1522, Anne Boleyn returned to England from the Netherlands to marry James Butler, 9th Earl of Ormond, who she had been betrothed to. For some unknown reason, their marriage never happened; and Anne was soon in need of a future husband. When she was installed as *Maid of Honour* to the Queen's consort, and in daily presence of the royal family, Anne had quickly caught the King's eye. And as soon as he had made up his mind that he wanted Anne Boleyn to be his mistress, he began to take the first steps to insure it would materialise.

The following year Anne Boleyn was secretly betrothed to Henry Percy, 6th Earl of Northumberland: a young military officer who had apparently fallen in love with her. The King was being informed weekly of every detail in Anne Boleyn's daily life; and when this news reached him he had an established member of his Privy Council, Thomas Wolsey, sent to influence the young officer to make him end his betrothal. Wolsey returned successful; and in 1526 Henry Percy married a different woman whom he had been interested in for many years, called Mary Talbot.

Towards the end of 1523, Henry made an informal visit to see Anne Boleyn at her stately home, Hever Castle. Her father implored Anne to remain upstairs during the King's visit. This was because Henry had already had Mary Boleyn, Anne's sister, as his mistress, which neither resulted in marriage or any betterment of status for the Boleyns' – something her father sought earnestly, and saw his daughters as a means to achieve it (not that they had anything against their father's wish, but may not have been as keen as he was to become so well acquainted with the King). Thomas withheld Henry from seeing Anne that day to subvert him, and to say in an offhand way: 'If you want Anne, it will be on *my* terms ...'

Having roused the King's determined mindset, *Anne Boleyn* would become his sole object to be attained. The years that followed Henry spent in lustful angst pursuing his new found love.

Henry VIII

ANNE BOLEYN'S GHOST

Poem by Henry VIII

Alas! What shall I do for love? For love, alas! What shall I do? Sith now so kind, I do you find, To keep you me unto. Alas!

In summer of 1530 fifteen clerics and one proctor from Canterbury were prosecuted by the King's council for adhering to Wolsey's papal legacy on grounds of Praemunire: the offense of obeying a foreign power and not the sovereign. Henry wanted the title of *'Sole protector and supreme head of the English church and clergy'*. The trial was delayed for one year; and when it recommenced the clergy hammered out a deal with Henry, and he would have the title he wished for; but not without compromise. After giving in to a one hundred thousand pound offer from the clergy (a colossal sum at the time, equivalent to a tenth of the church's entire wealth), he had dropped most of the charges, and accepted the title with the small print: *'as far as Christ's laws allows,'* added to it.

In autumn of 1531 a small mob attacked Anne Boleyn at a dinner party in a house situated along the River Thames. The mob, made up mostly of women, as well as some men, apparently wanted to harm or even kill her. Catherine of Aragon was still much loved by the people; and when word spread that the King was maneuvering to remove her, and that Anne Boleyn was the reason for it, tensions were bound to rise. Fortunately for Anne, she was hurried into a boat and rowed to the opposite side of the river before any harm could be done.

The incident unsettled and angered her: she was never attacked *before* she met Henry, and now a group of complete strangers seemed bent on killing her. She thought: *'If indeed I am putting my life in danger by being seen with the King, why didn't he send guards to protect me? Or am I of such little worth he could care less if I'm dead...?'* Perhaps it was an innocent mistake on his part; though he soon wished he hadn't, as he got the full force of her upset when he next saw her.

When she had finally voiced her shaken sentiments emotively to the King, he felt somewhat perplexed by her unrestrained outburst at him, which produced a sense of unfamiliarity of being talked to in such a manner by his mistress; he, who expected nothing more from Anne than obedience, subservience, and a willingness to fulfill his will. And as Anne and Henry spent more and more time in others' presence, Anne undoubtedly added to that sense of *un*familiarity by being reserved in the one thing that would have kept the King *happy* ... however, Anne Boleyn saw herself not as a mere mistress, that Henry could be cast to one side, once the flame of passion had lost its brightness – but as the future *Queen of England,* so she had to play her cards *wisely*.

On September 1st, 1532 at Windsor Castle, Henry took the first step to make Anne Boleyn 'Queen' with a ceremony to ennoble her. It was a taste of things to come, and it took place in front of the Imperial Ambassador, the Dukes of Norfolk and Suffolk, and the Countess's of Rutland and Sussex. England was a feudal country; rank and title belonged to those men who were willing and able to fight for the King. In order for Anne Boleyn's status to rise, her father's had to rise as well: so Thomas Boleyn duly became the Earl of Wiltshire, while Anne's title became Marquis of Pembroke, accompanied by a yearly income of a thousand pounds that came from the new lands and manors she now owned.

Henry had been wrestling with his marriage to Catherine of Aragon for some time. He wanted it ended, and had been spending most of his energy devising a way out of it; universities throughout Europe were called on to give their opinion on the matter. Because Catherine was previously betrothed to Henry's brother Arthur, he would refer to Leviticus and Deuteronomy to argue his marriage to her was unlawful. He sought papal recognition for what he saw as breaking *Gods Laws* by being married to her; even though he was not childless and had a healthy daughter born by her.

But a daughter wasn't what he had wished for ... *Nothing would do but a male heir to the throne.*

Catherine of Aragon

Later that year Anne Boleyn accompanied the King on one of his grand ships heading for France. Henry wanted to speak with Francis the First; and there were concerns whether Anne could be received with him, once there. The decision was made to stop in Calais – then English soil – and have her stay there until he returned.

On his return to Calais their journey back to England was postponed by a tempest. As they waited for the storm to subside, Anne finally gave in and admitted Henry to her bed.

*

Back in England, Anne and Henry were in the courtyard of Hever Castle, when Anne whispered in Henry's ear she was pregnant. There was a twinkle in one of the King's beetle-like eyes, and a small finch appeared out of nowhere and landed on one of his broad shoulders. Anne laughed as he failed to take notice, and was instead looking dreamily into space, like a man lost in wonder.

Unless they were officially married before the child's birth, the baby would be deemed illegitimate and unable to inherit the throne. Henry quickly began to get everything in to place; and considering what obstacles he had in his way, there was no time to lose. The Vatican was informed, but the response was taking far too long to reach England. The wedding *had* to take place without the pope's consent; and to do that, it had to take place in secret to avoid any public protest, or retaliation from Spain, or Rome.

Early in the day on January 25th, 1533 the wedding took place at Whitehall. Members of the Boleyn family attended the secretive wedding, as well as members of the King's Privy Council. It was not the most glamorous of weddings, having been both rushed and understated, coming at a time of necessity rather than convenience. However, attempts to keep the marriage a secret were successful; and for nearly a year after not a single person of authority or head of state knew anything about it. As the months grew and Anne found herself being treated better than she could ever remember, the secrecy of the marriage and pregnancy had been, ever so slightly, *weighing on her*.

Chapter VII

The Break from Rome

On October 1st, 1532 the letter had finally arrived from the Vatican and the Pope disapproved of Henry's wish to marry Anne Boleyn. Included in the letter was a written order demanding Henry to stop seeing Anne, and to take back Catherine of Aragon. In an attempt to blackmail Henry, the Pope had then threatened to excommunicate him from the Roman Catholic Church if he failed to conform to the order. In effect, the Vatican had usurped its authority over England; and in turn, Henry would usurp his grip on power with ground-shaking results.

This action and reaction acted like a slingshot: the bands having been tightened could no longer be pulled; all that could happen was for all that energy to be released in one, sudden, violent *snap*. In the same letter was a confirmation of Thomas Cranmer's new title as Archbishop of Canterbury. Capitalizing on this confirmation of one of his men in to a position of power, Cranmer was made to give an oath of allegiance to the King, to God, but *not* to the Pope, if it involved breaking the law of the land, or going against the will of the King. He was publicly consecrated in St. Stephen's Church on March 30th, 1533.

It became paramount to have Henry's marriage to Catherine annulled; and, as soon as possible, to have his marriage to Anne Boleyn recognized by all England. Cranmer was soon granted increased powers by Parliament. Everything was set: Anne Boleyn would be crowned Queen. But the road ahead was far from smooth. Francis the First was swiftly informed, while Catherine of Aragon was sent a signed order demanding her to give up the royal jewels, cease using the title of 'Queen', and to accept her new title as *Dowager Princess of Wales*. She refused to budge. Adamant all was being wrought by the so called 'Concubine' Catherine continued to use her prestigious title, and expected those who addressed her to do *exactly* the same. Outraged, Henry ordered his footmen to move her to a place where she would be of little annoyance, and restricted her from seeing her daughter Mary, until she accepted his terms. Nothing dissuaded her; the title of *Queen* would prove to be too much to part with.

Out in the lonely English country, deprived of her riches and her fame, she became delusional, increasingly sensational, and insisted that her few servants continue to embroider their new cloths with Henry's and Catherine's initials.

May 10th, 1533 the Blackfriars Court gave its verdict on Henry's marriage to Catherine of Aragon; they concluded he had never been married to Catherine; and as a bachelor, he had married Anne Boleyn *legally*. Anne was now, in some sense, the Queen; and her child would be the rightful heir to the throne. All the trouble Henry had gone to, had paid off; and to make up for Anne's lackluster wedding, he promised that her coronation was going to be something *extraordinary*.

Chapter VIII

The Coronation

May 29th, 1533 Anne Boleyn was preparing for her coronation at Greenwich Palace. Five months' pregnant, a healthy bump was clearly visible on her. Dressed in cloth of gold, her hair fell below her waist; and the royal jewels gleamed brightly over her elegant frame under the enchanting sky.

Gliding down the River Thames, Anne's barge led the way as an array of other barges drifted close by – her symbolic emblem of a white falcon rising from a bed of Tudor rose's clear to be seen from each side of the River Thames – as well as hundreds of smaller lavishly adorned boats; and musicians crowded the decks to provide a fruitful abundance of joyful music. Each barge was uniquely decorated with wreaths of flowers, colourful ribbons, and had been polished to shine for the occasion.

At around five o'clock the cannons boomed, the guns pealed, and the trumpets roared as Anne Boleyn approached the Tower of London. Once she had docked, Anne was warmly greeted and with many emphatic nods and bows by the Tower's various staff, before being led straight to the King by the Tower's constable, William Kingston, and the Mayor of London.

Henry showed fervid affection for Anne when she appeared: her dazzling form producing awe and wonder inside him. Smiling, Henry got to his feet, approached her enthusiastically, and wrapped his large arms around her in a pincer-like grip. Attempting to be gentle through his excitement, as he kept in mind the delicate child inside her, he loosened his grasp; Anne's face glowing scarlet by the time he did. What wasn't there to be happy about? Everything was running smoothly: *just like clockwork.*

That evening a mighty dinner party was held, which included eighteen specially selected guests, all of whom were about to be anointed knights, foods that appealed to every taste, and plenty of music.

The following Saturday, on the streets of London, Anne Boleyn was accompanied by a convoy of nobles of the realm, made up of Gentries, Knights, Members of Parliament and dignitaries, on horseback from the Tower of London to Westminster Palace. Everywhere she looked there were large banners inscribed with Henry's and Anne's initials *'HA'*, newly settled coats of paint in lively vibrant colours; flowers of immense variety; and silver and gold ornaments adorned every square foot of the pageant. Four Knights of the Five Ports held a canopy of estate above her head; the Archbishop of Canterbury later commented on it saying: 'She sitting in her hair, upon a horse litter.' Cloth of silver lined the beautiful well-bred horses.

After Anne came four magnificent chariots. The first was empty, and the three others had distinguished women in them, called divers; they were followed by a large assembly of yet more women. The whole convoy extended nearly half a mile in length, and wine was made available at various conduits spanning the pageant. Men, women and children looked on and waved as Anne Boleyn passed them; but although every effort had been made to make the day a pleasant one, there was no hiding the deathly silence that followed her as she moved slowly through the streets of London, masked only by the trotting hooves of the horses and the turning of carriage wheels ... England was falling out with Rome, and if the strings continued to loosen, all that could come of it was decades of uncertainty and rivalry throughout the land.

The procession ended at Westminster Hall, where a banquet had been prepared for her. After the feast, Anne exited at the back of the palace which lead out on to the River Thames, entered her barge, and was promptly rowed to York Place, which brought an end to the day's events.

Next day Anne Boleyn was crowned *Queen of England*.

Archbishop of Canterbury, Thomas Cranmer

THE CORONATION

This is a revised version of Thomas Cranmer's first-hand account of the momentous day, which he wrote in a letter to Mr. Hawkins, English Ambassador at the court of the Emperor, Charles the Fifth:

On Sunday June 1st, Anne left Whitehall, the destination being Westminster Abbey. At Westminster Church the Bishops of Lincoln, London, Bath, York, Winchester, St. Asaph, and I, had all assembled and were preparing for the coronation, along with the Abbot of Westminster and about ten other Abbot's. The Bishop's and Abbot's followed me out of the Abbey, and then we proceeded towards Westminster Hall, carrying the crosses and crosiers. In a procession we entered Westminster Hall, and received the Queen and all the ladies that accompanied her. The Queen was wearing a robe of purple velvet, and the ladies around her were in scarlet robes and gowns. The Bishops of London and Winchester were standing at either side of her; she in her hair; my lord of Suffolk holding the crown in front of her, and two other lords also stood near to him holding a scepter and a white rod. They proceeded up into the High Altar, and the ceremonies took place. I set the crown upon her head, and then we sung Te Duem. After that, a solemn mass took place while her Grace sat crowned upon a scaffold, which was made between the High Altar and the choir in Westminster Church. With the Mass and ceremonies done and finished, all of the assembly of noblemen brought her into Westminster Hall again, where a great solemn feast awaited her; the good dinner was much too long for me to put into words.

Chapter IX

Elizabeth Arrives

Anne was approaching eight months' pregnant, and was spending most of her time within the grounds at Greenwich Palace. Henry, meanwhile, was passing the time hunting in Windsor, making short trips there to enjoy his much loved sport – or so Anne thought; apparently, there was another 'sport' the King was quite fond of. With Anne being physically less attractive and a stomach larger than a melon, while Henry was away he had an affair with a woman who was all too ready to befriend *'His Majesty'*.

By the time this news reached Anne, she was starting to go into labour, and could worry little about her husband's unfaithfulness with the anxiety of childbirth hanging over her. When Henry finally returned from Windsor, Anne gave vent to what she had heard. He casually responded by telling her not to make a fuss: that it was all nonsense and *lies*.

On September 7th, 1533 Anne Boleyn gave birth to a beautiful baby girl. At that moment the excitement and *expectation* for a boy had been all but destroyed, and everybody in the Boleyn family knew how devastated the King would be if Anne could not provide him with a male heir. Nasty looks met her everywhere she went: if Anne failed to give birth to the child the King wished for, it would not only affect his behavior toward her, but would be a detriment to them all: and for this Anne was already feeling the *ill will* from those closest to her. At first, Henry reacted calmly; deep down a fire began to kindle within him. 'She *will* have brothers,' he said avidly.

There were strong signs for hope. The baby was healthy; and the time Anne had spent in labour had had few moments of worry. Their new daughter, who they named *Elizabeth*, was seen at her christening wearing a purple robe of velvet; her train so long four Lords were needed to carry it.

Henry's older daughter, Mary, now became of some concern. Steps were taken to insure Elizabeth's status for the future, but rivalry between them was going to be unavoidable. The King had made his new daughter the heir to the throne, despite the fact she wasn't the boy he so he so desperately wanted. *Something* about Elizabeth made Henry look twice at her.

Five years later Henry would be borne a son by Jane Seymore, who he promptly made his heir to the throne. When the young Lady Elizabeth was told of the change she said: 'How haps it, Governor, yesterday my Lady Princess, and today but my Lady Elizabeth?'

Elizabeth I

March, 1534 Anne fell pregnant again. Sometime between then and January the following year, she had the fatal *miscarriage*. The King's confidence in his wife's ability to deliver him healthy children, with the first being so healthy and full of life, had given him the misled idea that it would be safe to try for another child, so soon after Anne's first successful pregnancy. And shortly after her first miscarriage, she fell pregnant and miscarried again in June.

With two failed pregnancies under her belt, patience was beginning to wear thin; the King's temper worse than Anne had ever seen it (which was quite an achievement for Henry): his eyes bulging frighteningly out of their sockets, as things once again seemed not to be going the way he had planned.

Anne's family was all too aware that their marriage had been deteriorating, ever since Elizabeth had arrived. However, Henry had not yet given up hope. He was sure Anne would *eventually* give birth to another healthy baby; and could only hope that when she did, it would be the boy he was after. The thought that this might not happen, he buried deep for another day, determined to give Anne a bit more time to prove she was indeed worthy of his hand.

The King brought the Act of Succession before parliament, which made Elizabeth's title harder to dispute; and in the event that Anne did give birth again, her child would be acknowledged as legitimate without question. This was soon followed by an attempt to pass the Act of Supremacy – a far more controversial proposal – which prevented the sending of revenues to Rome, would make Henry the Supreme Head of the Church of England, and would all but sever the Church of England from the Church of Rome.

The storm had been in their midst for more than a century, but in 1534 it began to *rumble*.

Chapter X

The King's Will

When Pope Clement died in September that year, Henry tried to negotiate with his successor, Paul the Third. He told him he would reverse his decision, and that England would continue to be intrinsically tied with Rome, if he would accept his marriage to *Anne Boleyn*. But Pope Paul, like Clement and Julius before him, did not heed to Henry's request; and to top off his unreasoning attitude, he made John Fisher, a long time supporter of Henry's first wife, a cardinal.

Thomas More was a respected lawyer and avid supporter of Catherine of Aragon. He was known as a social philosopher, a writer, and an opponent of the Protestant Reformation. He, like many others, simply would not accept Henry as '*Supreme Head of the Church of England*'; and soon the King would find out just how far they would be willing to go to stop him.

During a sermon, the King declared under the 'Cannons of the Apostles' he had High Power under God, and ought to be the Supreme Head over all spiritual prelates. As the King prayed he exclaimed: 'Ye shall pray for the Universal Church of all Christendom, and especially for the prosperous estate of our sovereign and *Emperor King Henry the Eight*, being the only Supreme Head of this realm of England.'

More and Fisher felt so strongly against the Act of Supremacy, they were willing to risk their own lives contesting it. And they were by no means alone. Numerous monasteries, priories, churches, and scholars all had something to say about the Act; and a feeling of indignation had roused in them all. This unwillingness, up and down the land, to conform to the King's will, infuriated him; and soon he would resort to the one core element of his reign: the men who empowered him: the Royalists – his Army.

Henry VIII: 'There is no head so fine but I will make it fly.'

Key establishments throughout England, Wales, and Ireland were about to be destroyed and lost forever. Some of the greatest priories, churches, and cathedrals were reduced to nothing more than ash and rubble. It was to be one of the most infamous demonstrations of power a king has forced upon his own kingdom; and the scars from the destruction that followed are still visible today.

First on the list were the Carthusians, an influential Roman Catholic monastic order. The priests and priors were rounded up from their communities and taken to the Tower of London, where they were swiftly imprisoned, tried, and sentenced. They were then sent to the village of Tyburn, where the sentences were duly carried out.

One by one they were hanged. As death neared, the rope from which they hung was cut. Finally the victim was dragged to the spot where he or she was disemboweled, before their organs were set ablaze in front of their fading eyes ...

*

John Fisher and Thomas More would not accept the Act of Supremacy in its entirety, even after all of the bloodshed. Shortly after the executions at Tyburn, Fisher was beheaded at the Tower of London. His head was placed on a spike and advertised from Tower Bridge, for all London to goggle at. The head loomed there for months with not the slightest signs of rot. Birds didn't feed on it, and not a single maggot fell from it.

One dull grey day a local tradesman, who was passing the bridge, stopped and stared awhile at Fisher's unchanging head; and having long heard people talk suspiciously of Fisher's head on his way to work, or at work, as if it was some kind of supernatural omen, he climbed up the bridge, yanked the head off its spike, and threw it in the River Thames. And when considering Londoners in the sixteenth century were more than used to seeing decapitated heads on their daily commute or birds flying to and fro with eyeballs or other *fleshy* thing in their beaks – Fisher's head caused quite a stir at the time.

Thomas More was given an extra month to accept the Act of Supremacy. This was mainly due to the King's likeness of More, who Henry knew well, and had even considered him to be a friend at one time; they used to play tennis together.

In July that year, More was executed at the Tower. Before the axe fell he said: 'I die the King's good servant, but God's first.'

Chapter XI

Untimely Mishap

In the summer of 1535 the King and Queen travelled to the edge of Wales seeking to brighten their spirits. Summer was a time when sickness and disease in London was rife. The Black Death still existed in England; though much less severe than it had been a few centuries before; and it was wise to get away from the capital if you could. That autumn, whilst in the serene surroundings of the Welsh countryside, Anne fell pregnant for the final time.

When, to everyone's sheer disbelief, Catherine of Aragon died, before a single word was said by either Anne or Henry, the sense of a burden having been lifted from his shoulders overcame him: she was one less thing to worry about; her ties with Henry were now completely undone. One of the royal servants described, in a measured tone, how the embalmer, who had worked on Catherine's corpse, had noticed a black lump in her throat; and when he had inspected her heart, he found it was also black. Had she poisoned herself, in despair of losing all that she had held dear? Or did Henry order to have her secretly killed, for having given him a hard time when he wanted a divorce?

On January 27th, 1534 – the day Catherine's funeral was scheduled for – the King decided to spend the day, not in mourning her death, but rather he did the complete opposite, and made the day something to *celebrate*. Held at Greenwich Palace, Henry rode triumphantly towards the jousting tournament, and was eager to begin. Loud cheers unsettled the quiet landscape all round as the King appeared on the ridge above the gathered spectators and combatants. Dense snowy-white clouds filled the sky, with small gaps of blue tunneling through them now and again, like great eyes. Anne, who was three months' pregnant, had retired in the palace, and was keeping well away from the rowdy atmosphere of the *Joust*.

Henry suited up in his riding armour and mounted his competition horse, with the help of his staff, who strained under the growingly obese man (his armour almost doubling his already enormous weight). A gunshot sounded and they were off, each gaining speed as they thundered headlong towards the other – the King shifting himself in his saddle all the while, trying to find a strong hold of his lance through the ensuing turbulence. His opponent, however, rode gallantly at him, locking his lance in place with seemingly mechanical ease.

Henry tried to mirror his opponent, but to no avail; and after a desperate lunge of his prong, a mighty *thwack* unhorsed the King with such unforgiving force, he was immediately rendered unconscious; and lumbered towards the ground, unearthing heaps of dirt as he violently came to a stop. He lay motionless on the torn earth, segments of his broken armour scattered all around him.

Hundreds of feet pounded the earth as everyone in the crowd ran to the scene; and there they met a worrying site: *Henry lay still as death*. Carefully, those around him began to remove bits of dented and dirt-laden armour from his stout frame, while a physician scanned him intensively checking to see if had suffered a fatal blow. Countless times they tried to see if he was still breathing, but it was almost impossible to tell. One hour had passed, and still the King lay motionless under the solemn sky. Everybody knew it: the King was dead; and Anne's uncle sought to give her the tragic news.

* * *

On having been told of Henry's accident, the shock affected her to such a degree she had the dreaded miscarriage that day. Anne's spirits were in anguish. As she lay on her bed, distraught and in pain, peering through a panned window as night descended heavily upon the lifeless grounds, trees groaned in the wind and rain, their contorted spear-like branches glistening threateningly in the dark and snapping at the odd gale. Anne could only hope this horrific day was over.

All of a sudden she saw a menacing shadow moving and growing larger in the flicker of torchlight outside her room. A feeling of foreboding twisted inside her: the somberness of the day had become worryingly *charged*. Everyone within the palace seemed stifled in their tracks: Henry had gained consciousness and his strength, and was being hastily led through the halls to the Queen. Anne hurried to her bed and cowered there; Henry's heavy footsteps hammered the floor as he approached her room, shaking glass on tables and dislodging pictures in their frames. She was dreading Henry's reaction to the miscarriage, more than being relieved he was alive and well – and it being on top of his near-fatal accident seemed to make it all the worse.

When Henry entered her room, he had a maniacal air about him as he looked virulently at his ailing wife, not uttering a single word or phrase whilst all the time strangely transfixed on Anne's dark eyes. His demeanor said what his voice would not: That I, your master, stand before you, *dear*, having woken from my 'long nap' only to find you have miscarried, *again!*

When Anne did try and speak – the shock of his presence having set her nerves on fire – he interrupted her before she could start.

'I –'

'*I* see clearly that God does not wish to give me male children …' Henry said; and, falling silent, he walked over to the window and gazed blankly before him. Anne remained quiet and frozen in her bed, and dared not speak.

As the silence went on and on, seeing he was lost for words, Anne meekly approached the window, wishing to comfort him in his fretfulness, when he said decisively: '*You will get no more sons by me!*' He took leave of her room; Anne weeping despairingly as he went.

Henry's loyalty to Anne was diminishing as quickly as it had flourished. He soon began to consult his new chief minister, Thomas Cromwell, on the best way of getting *rid* of Anne Boleyn. The King was determined to avoid another questionable divorce, or be humiliated with yet another public scandal. He needed to make the woman he went to so much trouble to be with, appear to be someone he completely mistook for being sophisticated and charming, and who was, underneath it all, a whore –

After many long arduous nights alone in his bed, thinking how best to bring about his master's wish, Cromwell's strategy was to have Anne proven guilty of treason; and the only way he could do that was to prove she had committed adultery: the only woman in England who could be executed on such a charge. That's not to say the task Cromwell had set himself was one that was going to be easy to achieve; but being a somewhat scrupulous individual, Cromwell could get done almost anything he set his mind to.

Chapter XII

Devising a Plan

In the sixteenth century, it was all but impossible for someone like the King or Queen to get away with the odd affair, without the knowledge of those in their circle. They were the celebrities of their day; rumour and gossip was to the people who knew them, the equivalent of today's news media, celebrity magazines, and newspapers.

Cromwell invited a musician called Mark Smeaton over for a very special, one-to-one dinner with him at his home in Stepney. Smeaton was the ideal man to achieve the King's aim. As a talented musician, who could play several instruments and sing, Anne had requested on some occasions for Smeaton to perform in the royal household. He lacked friends and family, and had no influence beyond the stage. All that was needed now was a bit of 'persuasion', and that's where Cromwell came in.

Thomas Cromwell

As soon as Smeaton had arrived in Stepney and stepped out of his carriage (kindly provided for by the King), Cromwell went to his front window and beckoned him in. Smeaton meandered his way inside, and sat down at the table where a few dishes had been prepared for him to tuck into.

There was duck and pheasant (both well roasted and slightly charred), grapes, apples, chestnuts; and one bottle of wine, which Cromwell prowled over as if his guest's lips might infect its contents. Cromwell sat quietly, the tips of his short stubby fingers together, observing Smeaton intently with his beady black eyes. Smeaton looked somewhat tense, and was hopelessly trying to hide it behind mouthfuls of Cromwell's victuals.

After ten minutes, Cromwell asked if Smeaton was enjoying his cooking; and before he could ask him anything else, Smeaton began chatting freely with the highly educated Cromwell, by talking about the pleasant weather, and focusing on his musical talents: expecting that was the reason why he had been invited to dine with him – he had brought along his violin, *just in case.*

Cromwell seemed pleased to hear a tune or two, and smiled widely as he played; though it soon contorted itself into a sneer, as Smeaton prowess led him on and on. Cromwell began to mutter, averting his eyes to his blissfully at home guest. 'Shut up now ... Smeaton –' said Cromwell, the blood now rushing to his head. Smeaton obviously hadn't been taught the meaning of: '*SHUT UP*' – or perhaps he couldn't hear them, through the loudness of his concerto.

Half an hour later Smeaton suddenly ceased playing: he had finally noticed the sour look on Cromwell's face. He took up his glass and resumed eating, trying hard to avoid Cromwell's fathomless eyes. The long silence was broken as Cromwell attempted to converse with his very awkward guest. With a hint of cynicism in his voice, he told Smeaton what a skillful musician he was, and talked a bit about the time he learned to play the harpsichord: how he never could get to grips with it, because of his fat fingers (holding them up so Smeaton could admire them for their *im*perfectness). Smeaton laughed. Cromwell glared back at him.

After an hour had gone by, and a few more goblets of wine had been swallowed, Cromwell began to insinuate the reason why he had wanted to speak with him. He asked Smeaton, rather bluntly, whether 'Her Grace' had taken him to her bed. Smeaton reacted like someone who had just heard a sentence in a foreign language. As he stared and blinked into

DEVISING A PLAN

oblivion, Cromwell said that he had been informed by one of Her Grace's servants of some 'mischievous goings-on', which had taken place, late at night, while Smeaton was in her house.

Smeaton grew increasingly confused at this: scratching his head and seemingly lost for all words. Occasionally, he would open his mouth, like a baby on the verge of saying its first word; but merely breathed and continued looking perplexedly at his host. Finally, after the longest and most painful silence Cromwell had endured in his life, Smeaton asked if it was some sort of a joke, and forced a small laugh, acting like he had taken awhile to get the gist of it.

Again, Cromwell stared at him with his beady black eyes, took a swig of wine from its goblet, and dug his dirty nails into an apple he had recently picked up, before taking a large wet bite. 'Do you like Her Grace?' he said smoothly, after emptying his glass and devouring his apple.

'*Very* much ... well, I did – I mean ...'

'You did? Explain. Hast thou *ill feeling* towards Her Grace?' Cromwell's gaze hardened, and the colour in Smeaton's face drained white.

'It's nothing ... nothing at all, re—'

'Come on. Spit it out!'

Smeaton stammered for some time, trying to find his tongue. At last, he said that Her Grace had been unkind to him some time ago. Looking as if he was trying to find the right words he mouthed a few words, but there was no noise. But then his face turned a curious shade of reddish-purple, and he swelled up and shouted '*SHE'S A HEARTLESS W—*' Breathing heavily and feeling he had gone quite far enough, his voice fell away; though Cromwell had a good idea what he was about to say. Cromwell knew all about Smeaton's infatuation for Anne Boleyn, which Mark would never admit to a soul, though it was apparent to practically everyone who knew him. Cromwell was elated to hear this and waited to spring his trap, upon which he casually stated, as if it had been long rehearsed: 'There's no need to feel like the hare being chased by the fox. His Grace is of a most beneficent nature, and would be grateful for any *honest* man who gave evidence regarding Her Grace's *abhorrent* conduct; and will reward him *rightly* on his degree of – er – *helpfulness*.'

'But as for those who stand in the King's way,' Cromwell informed him, 'he can be the most merciless creature to walk the earth.' And he scowled with animation as he said this.

Smeaton looked warily around him. Cromwell stood up, took a few small steps forward, patted Mark on the shoulder, and said softly, 'You know what to do ... Don't let it be *thy* head –'

He led Smeaton outside, and without so much as a *good-bye* he looked on as Smeaton wandered off; and as Cromwell placed his hand on the door Smeaton glanced over his shoulder: Cromwell drew a finger across his throat, smiled menacingly, and slammed the door shut behind him. Smeaton walked clumsily away.

The following week Smeaton had confessed to committing adultery with Anne Boleyn, and had named four other men who he said had done the same. With the desired confession attained, and more, Smeaton was taken to the Tower of London to be held prisoner, while a messenger was sent to Greenwich to give the King the 'good news'.

*

It was May Day at Greenwich Palace, and there was that familiar sense of electricity in the air as on that turbulent unforgettable day of the jousting tournament. It was a sunny and windy day, and once again a jousting tournament was the main entertainment at the palace (though today the King was content to watch from afar, with seemingly more important matters to attend to).

Later that day, Anne heard several horses' hooves shifting gravel in the courtyard at the front of the palace. She went to the window and saw Henry and six other men mounting their horses and exiting the grounds at a gallop. There was a sense of urgency to their departure, and Anne quickly sought information regarding the King's sudden leave.

With no insight coming from any of her staff, at around four o'clock the Queen went to enjoy the festival, hoping to keep her mind off her husband. Lots of noise was still coming from the jousting tournament, so she stopped there first, receiving several bows and curtseys as she passed. Growing tired of the sound of clashing steel, Anne made her way towards the lively music, where she found people dancing and eating happily outside around several bonfires. Hearty foods were being cooked: pigs were roasting on spits and stews were bubbling lazily in cauldrons; the smells permeating in the fresh slightly-mild air. Couples could be seen hiding behind trees, where they kissed; and children ran around playing with one another or having make-believe duels with wooden swords. Anne looked on and took in the sights and smells for some time, when suddenly her eyes fell upon the fire nearest her as the sounds around her seemed to drift miles away; lively silky flames danced betwixt the jovial faces all around it, shining brightly on each like a spotlight; as if their souls could never fade, never worry.

As the sun descended below the horizon, and the thought of Henry surfaced again, Anne made her way back to the palace, to see if any news regarding him had finally arrived. Meanwhile, the accused men Smeaton had named had all been arrested, and were being questioned at the Tower of London. Sir Henry Norris was mortified by the charges put him. Utterly amazed and outraged by what he was being accused of, he requested to dual with the King in defense of Anne's honour and his own. Sir Francis Weston was knighted the day before Anne was crowned Queen, and now a dire fate awaited him as he tried to contest his innocence amongst the King's corrupt court. William Brereton and Lord Rochford (Anne's brother!) were the two others Smeaton had named. All of them vehemently denied the charges.

Chapter XIII

Losing Her Freedom

May 2nd, 1536 Anne Boleyn was taken, under arrest, to meet with the King's Privy Council at Westminster Palace, to begin proceedings. Thomas Cromwell, the Duke of Norfolk, and two others waited for her arrival.

Once she was seated and in full gaze of the Privy Council, Anne stared fixedly at them, interested to know their reasons for summoning her. There was a long silence. Finally the Duke said one-tonally, that Mark Smeaton, a Court Musician, and Henry Norris, Groom of the Stool, had confessed at the Tower of London to having committed adultery with Anne Boleyn. In reality, only Smeaton had confessed; and by claiming Henry Norris had done so as well, the Council was hoping to put Anne on weak footing, and to dig in the injustice that was unfolding before her very eyes.

Aghast at what she was hearing, Anne fervently denied the charges read her, which filled her soul with disgust at the mere mention of them. The Duke paused, having witnessed her calm, dignified reaction, looked at her cynically and said: *'Tut, tut, tut,'* shaking his head in a slow sickly heavy manner.

Thomas Howard, 3rd Duke of Norfolk

With the tide turning against the Boleyns', everyone in it was out for their own necks. Back at Greenwich Palace, at around five o'clock that evening, Anne was waiting to be sent to the Tower, and was being treated more like a criminal, than the *Queen of England*.

Sailing along the River Thames, all was quiet except for the oars as they creaked and groaned in their locks, and the rustling of water beneath them. Storm clouds loomed above.

Arriving at the same spot where she had entered the Tower on her coronation day, three years prior, Anne Boleyn was once again kindly received by the Tower's constable, William Kingston. He appeared sombre today; and when Anne's boat docked he offered her his hand as she placed her feet on to the Tower's cold stone. Overcome with grief, Anne fell to her knees, horror-struck. 'Shall I go into a dungeon?' she asked Kingston, wiping her tears and coming to her feet.

'No, no, Madam,' he said; 'to the chamber that you lay in before your coronation.'

Anne's attendants were forbidden to speak in her presence, and were ordered to report anything she said directly to Cromwell. At the same time, the Treasurer of the King's house, Master Fittes-Williams, was ordered to break-up and depose her servants of their duties.

Behind the Tower's high encompassing walls, Anne looked up at the dark enclosing sky; something told her she would not be leaving them alive.

* * *

The eerie silence, only ever broken by woeful cries; the gravity of what she was being accused of, with execution being the likeliest form of punishment; and suddenly finding herself – *the Queen of England* – condemned to the Tower of London: the gloom of it seeped deeper with every passing second into her soul.

When the Archbishop of Canterbury heard what was happening, he quickly dispatched a letter to the King.

This is a revised version of the letter he wrote to Henry on May 3rd, 1536:

Please your most noble Grace should be spoken with. As you have not asked to see me, I dare not, contrary to the contents of the said letters presume to come unto your Grace's presence; nevertheless, it is my most bounden duty, I can do no less than most humbly admire you for your great wisdom, and by the assistance of God's help, somewhat to suppress the deep sorrow of your Grace's heart, and to take all adversities of God's hand both patiently and thankfully. I cannot deny that you hath great causes, many of which are of lamentable heaviness: and also that, in the wrongful estimation of the world, your honour of every part is highly touched (whether the things that commonly be spoken of are true or not), that I can't remember Almighty God having sent unto your Grace a similar occasion to test your constancy throughout, whether you can be content to take of God's hand, as well as things displeasant as pleasant. And if he find in your most noble heart an obedience to His Will, that you should, without expressing discontent or too much heaviness, accept all adversities, and thank Him when all things succeed of your will and liking, and no less procure his glory and honour; then I suppose you never did a thing more acceptable for Him, since you first governed this your realm.

And if it be true, what is reported of Her Grace, and the people have rightly estimated these things, they shouldn't regard any part of your honour to be affected, but her honour to be clearly of little worth. And I am so perplexed, that my mind is clean amazed, for I never had better opinion in women than I had in her; which makes me think that she should not deserve blame. And again, I think Her Grace would not have gone so far, except she had surely been culpable ... Now, I think that you know, next to your Grace, I was bound unto her of all creatures living. Therefore, I most humbly ask you, to suffer me in that, which is both God's law, nature, also her kindness binds me to; that is, that I may, with your favour, wish and pray for her, that she may declare herself inculpable and innocent. And if she is found culpable, considering your goodness towards her, and from what condition your only mere goodness took her, and set the crown upon her head; I repute Him not your faithful servant and subject, nor true to the realm, that would not desire the offence to be punished without mercy, to the example of all other. And as I did not love her, for the love which I judged to bear towards God and his gospel; so, if she proved culpable, there is not one that loves God and his gospel that will favour her, but must hate her above all other; and the more they favour the gospel, the more they will hate her: for then there was never a creature in our time that so much slandered the gospel. And God has sent her his punishment, for feigning to have professed his gospel in her mouth, and not in heart and deed. And although she would have offended, that she have deserved never to be reconciled in your favour; yet Almighty God has of many kinds declared his goodness towards you, and never offended you. But you, I am sure, will acknowledge that you have offended him. Therefore, I trust that you will bear no less but your entire favour for the truth of the gospel than you did before: as your favour of the gospel was not led by your affection of her, but your desire for the truth. And so I beseech Almighty God, whose gospel he has ordained you to be defender of, ever to preserve your Grace from all evil, and give you at the end promise of his gospel.

Though the letter is heavily worded with regard to Anne Boleyn, there was no denying the graveness of what she was being accused of. He was clearly performing a balancing act at the time he wrote this, at the same time being deeply shocked by the news. On the one hand, he felt it highly unlikely she was guilty, given the sacred role she carried out. On the other, he knew what lengths Henry went to get rid of his first wife, Catherine, when she had failed to give birth to a son; and no doubt this had happened again with Anne ... so whilst imploring the King to be truthful, as this time he was putting virtuous lives at stake (not something Henry took much concern over, if the people involved were an impediment to his will), and that he would be putting his own soul at great peril if lack of truth sufficed – if Cranmer didn't watch his words and play along with Henry, he would come down on him like a sack of stones if he thought his trust in him was wavering.

Chapter XIV

The Accused are Heard

May 12th, 1536 the trials had begun at Westminster Palace. Four of the five accused men were being heard by the King's Privy Council. Anne thought she knew the reason why Smeaton was so willing to tarnish her reputation, and was cursing herself for the day she believed had led, or had contributed, to the hopeless position she and five innocent men now found themselves in.

The real reason why she was being kept prisoner and possibly facing execution, there was no doubt: Henry sought to remove her, by any means necessary, as she had failed, like Catherine before her, to give birth to the child and heir that would have insured the family tradition of passing down the throne from father to son.

It was over a brief conversation that had taken place, when Anne had stopped by Smeaton in her home, and he was looking out of a window and appeared to be upset. It ran like this.

'I spoke with him on the Saturday before May Day,' she said. 'I found him standing in the round window in my chamber of presence, and I asked why he was so sad. He said: "It was no matter." Then I said: "You may not look to have me speak to you as I should to a nobleman, because you are an inferior person." And then he said: "No, no, Madam. A look sufficed me: and thus fare you well."'

Smeaton had longed for Anne Boleyn to notice him, ever since he had had the privilege of a being within her house. It was this plain inappropriateness, if not downright fool-heartedness, of Smeaton openly exhibiting his feelings for her at every chance he could, and Anne having sensed this for some time and feeling it was time to confront him, was what had made her react so snidely towards him that day. But it appears Smeaton didn't take her remark so well; and less than a month after Anne had insulted him (nevertheless spurred on by Cromwell), he was sitting before her in court, accusing her of having slept with him and four other men.

Anne went on to slander Smeaton openly for his falsehoods. She scorned him so severely and with unshakable fury, he lost all composure: his whole body shook, and his heels bounced energetically off the floor without rest. He could no longer manage to look at Anne Boleyn, nor the members of the Privy Council for that fact; but endeavored to engage them when spoken to, only to cower in his seat like a child who knows he has done something very wrong.

The accused were unable to say anything that might prove them guiltless. Now they could only wait to live out their fate, and be no more than puppets in the King's dark scheme. All of them, apart from Smeaton, were men of high nobility; yet it was Smeaton who was being given all the credibility of someone who had unquestionably high rank. All the accused had pleaded not guilty, as they found themselves not only charged with liaising salaciously with the highest woman in the land, but with plotting to kill the King as well!

With Anne no longer around, Henry's new lady in waiting was Jane Seymore. She was staying in a house situated along the River Thames, a little more than a stone's throw away from Westminster. After the day's tedious trials, Henry would get into a small boat and casually row himself up the River Thames to see Jane, who waited patiently for him to arrive at the home of Sir Nicholas Carew. Everything was once again going Henry's way; and he was eager to celebrate this turn of luck with his new mistress.

His covert trips up and down the river, however, didn't go unnoticed for long. Before he knew it, the locals had caught on to his nightly watery strolls, and, each evening, would look on from their homes as the King drifted slowly past, seemingly unaware to their protruding incredulous eyes.

In due course rumour spread, and soon it was the talk of London Town; before eventually the story made it as far away as Devon and Lincolnshire. The nation was wondering: '*Surely* the King isn't sneaking off during the trials, to have an affair with a *new* mistress, while the Queen is locked away and possibly facing execution on charges of *adultery?* Or could our leaders actually be so innately licentious...?'

This caused a gradual shift of feeling in favour of Queen Anne, as suspicion of the King – already deep-set since his first questionable divorce; had broken away from Rome; and had declared himself Head of the Church of England – firmly rooted itself in the land.

Four of the accused were sentenced by the Chancellor to be hanged, drawn and quartered (though their sentences were later changed to the less severe punishment of beheading, either because Henry had shown mercy on them as bitterness swelled all around him, or because of the wishes of the Archbishop). That foolish man, who went to have dinner

THE ACCUSED ARE HEARD

with Cromwell that day, had been betrayed; and soon he would be dragged from his dungeon, accompanied by Norris, Weston, Brereton an and Lord Rochford, to be beheaded for the base entertainment of the capital's populace.

Anne and George Boleyns' trials took place three days later, on May 15th, 1536. The public's knowledge of the King's secret nightly visits to his new mistress, while his imprisoned wife and *Queen* fought for freedom, brought in to question the King's motives, and of the validity of the charges against Anne Boleyn and those of nobility, which had been wrought by one petty individual of no distinct blood.

The Tower's officials had no choice but to rearrange where their trials would take place. Now there was too great a danger of a riot happening if Anne or George were moved from the secure walls of the Tower; therefore they would not be moved; they would be tried and sentenced within the *Tower of London*.

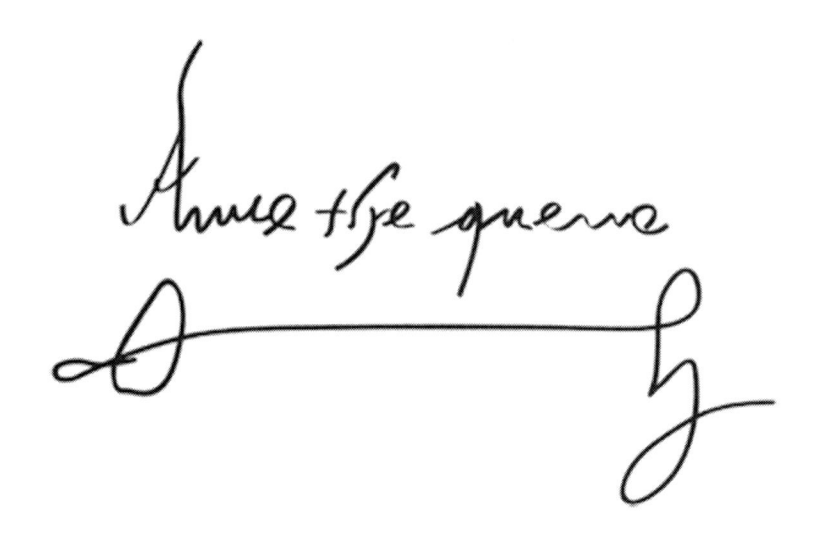

Anne Boleyn's Signature

*

On an elevated platform in the courtroom, a single chair was set for Anne Boleyn. The Court's peers of the realm had assembled. Twenty-six of them were selected by the King himself to pass judgment on Anne Boleyn; all of them had been chosen for their reliability to fulfill the King's agenda.

A knock on Anne's chamber-door announced Kingston's presence; a lieutenant waited quietly by his side. As he opened the door, Anne turned her eyes to Kingston; she seemed unaware he had knocked, and was sitting on her bed peering out the window on to the sodden hopeless grounds, apparently lost in thought, when he said, 'The Court waits, Madam …'

Having been led to the Great Hall, Anne Boleyn entered the cavernous dimly lit courtroom. She felt the weight of something ominous and bodeful all around her: it was almost suffocating her. The Lord Mayor of London, alderman and jury stood before her, and only sat back down again once she was seated. The Duke of Norfolk stood under the cloth of estate suspended prominently in the centre of the room, holding a grand richly-adorned white staffe and gazing malevolently all

THE ACCUSED ARE HEARD

the while at his niece. To his right, in the very centre of the room, stood the Duke of Suffolk, who was of higher rank than him; and to his right stood Lord Awdley, the Chancellor. In front of them stood the Earl of Surrey; his son and heir in front of him holding the golden staffe for the Earl Marshall. Everybody took their seats; and with Anne's grace and beauty lightening her uncle's blackened mind, he spat out the charges to her with relish.

'Despising her marriage and entertaining malice against the King and following daily her frail and carnal lust. On the 6th of October at the palace of Westminster, and various other days before and after, by sweet words, kissings, touchings and other illicit means, she did procure and incite, Sir Henry Norris, a gentlemen of the Privy Chamber of our lord the King, to violate and carnally know her, by reason whereof the same Henry Norris on October 12th violated and carnally knew her.

'Two counts of adultery took place on the 13th and 19th of May, 1534 with the said Mark Smeaton. Four counts of adultery took place on the 8th and 20th of May, and on the 6th and 20th of June, 1534 with the said Sir Francis Weston. Two counts of adultery took place on the 12th and 19th of November, 1533 with the said Sir Henry Norris. Four counts of adultery took place on thee –' a look of mock-disgust and loathing showed on his long pallid face as he rolled parchment lethargically, looking for the right dates '... oh yes; four counts of adultery took place on the 16th and 27th of November, and on the 3rd and 8th of December, 1533 with his lordship, Groom of the Privy Chamber, Sir William Brereton.

'And I mustn't forget,' said the Duke disdainfully '– three counts of incest with your brother, George Boleyn; all of which took place on the 22nd and 29th of December, the year of last.

'What does Her Grace *plea*?'

'I am *innocent* ...' Anne sighed and sensed the futility of her words, barely saying them loud enough for anyone to hear but herself.

'Does your Grace need the question to be uttered once more?' said the Duke of Suffolk after a long silence.

'*Not guilty!*' she cried.

The jurors glanced and murmured at one another as they came to their final verdict, causing a low uneven hum that echoed throughout the Hall; quick awkward glances were made at Anne, like shy school boys who were required to pass judgment on their teacher; and the emphatic shaking of heads by a handful of the jury, in a halfhearted attempt to portray their disbelief.

The Duke of Norfolk was given their verdict, and he methodically read the heartrending sentence to her.

Because thou hast offended against our sovereign the King's Grace in committing treason against his person, the law of the realm is this, that though hast deserved death and thy judgment is this: that thou shall be burnt here within the Tower of London on the green, else to have thy head smitten off, as the King's pleasure shall be further known of the same.

In the deathly silence that followed, Anne tried to come to terms with her fate. Her breast heaved as she struggled to restrain her sorrow. As her heart slowly began to settle inside her, and she came to a strange sense of calm, she breathed, 'Oh God, thou knoweth if I have merited this death.'

Addressing the Court that was now formless through her tearful eyes, Anne spoke. 'My Lords, I will not say your sentence is unjust, nor presume that my reasons can prevail against your convictions. I am willing to believe that you have sufficient reasons for what you have done: but they must be other than that which led you to this judgment, for I am clear of all the offences which you then laid to my charge. I have ever been a faithful wife to the King, though I do not say I have always shown him that humility which his goodness has to me, and thee honours to which he raised me, merited. I confess I have had jealous fancies and suspicions of him, which I had not discretion enough, and wisdom, to conceal at all times.

'Think not I say this in hope to prolong my life, for He who saveth from death hath taught me how to die, and He will strengthen my faith. Think not, however, that I am so bewildered in my mind as not to lay honour of my chastity to heart in mine extremity. When I have maintained it all my life long, much as ever as Queen I did.

'I know these, my last words, will avail me nothing but for the justification of my chastity and honour. As for my brother and those who were unjustly condemned, I would willingly suffer many deaths to deliver them, but since I see it so pleases the King, I shall willingly accompany them in death, with this assurance, that I shall lead an endless life with them in peace and joy, where I will pray to God for the King and for you, my Lords.' And far from floundering in her gait she rose from her chair and strode quietly out of the Hall, accompanied by Lady Kingston and Lady Boleyn at her side.

THE ACCUSED ARE HEARD

Prior to proceedings the King had ordered that all the documents produced during Anne Boleyn's trial were to be destroyed as soon as it had finished (though her indictment survived and is preserved in the Public Record Office, as well as a few writings that were apparently forgotten about in the home of Thomas Cromwell). It leaves no doubt that her trial was entirely void of merit.

George Boleyn's trial swiftly followed. As he was brought forward to the Great Hall he looked imploringly at Anne, trying to make eye contact with his ghostly white sister as she passed. Knowing he would suffer the same sombre fate, she didn't say a word; and only just acknowledged his presence by half-raising her tearful eyes to him, and walked soundlessly on.

Determined not to address the Court respectfully, as soon as George entered the Hall he cursed the wickedness of man. Incensed, his uncle stared at him with a poisoned expression on his face, and read the charges to him with a distinct growl in his throat.

'Thou has committed *incest* ... Thou has committed *treason* ... Thou has plotted to kill *the King!*'

There were rumours that the King might be impotent, but to suggest it would be considered a grave insult, and wouldn't go unpunished. George, however, was in the mood to have a stab at the King. In the end, he was fortunate not to suffer the cruelest death a man could be condemned to.

The Court's silence was shaken, and the jurors grumbled to one another as they decided what was to be his fate. His uncle hastily read their verdict and condemned him to be hanged, drawn quartered in the village of Tyburn. George was dragged from the Hall, writhing and shouting foul words of abuse at his wicked uncle as he went. His final days were spent behind the thick cold walls of the Tower deprived of food, water and light.

Chapter XV

Final Days

On May 17th, 1536 Smeaton, Norris, Brereton, Weston, and Lord Rochford were lead by the Yeomen Warders (nicknamed 'Beefeaters' because they were permitted to eat as much beef as they liked, on the King's purse) to the Block. Lord Rochford's sentence had been changed to beheading in the final hour: the King having been pleaded with by the Archbishop to show him mercy. Mark Smeaton was first in line, as he had pleaded guilty.

He almost walked himself on to the scaffold, and approached the headsman genially. And like a man of the theatre, Smeaton proclaimed to his audience: *'Masters, I pray thou shalt all pray for me, for I have deserved thee death!'* And without a glimmer of fear in his docile eyes he promptly positioned himself in place for the headsman standing silently and threateningly before him; though it didn't trouble Smeaton in the slightest, who seemed to be quite enjoying himself.

Bemused, the small chubby executioner picked at the blade of his axe with his thumb nail, and ran a finger lightly over the top as he felt for its sharpness. Looking down, he surveyed Smeaton, seeing where best to strike the blade on the back of his scrawny neck. Smeaton looked sideways to see if he was almost ready, as he had been taking awhile.

Then, without warning, the axe came storming down behind him, producing a low pitched *whoosh* as it broke the air around it. At long last Smeaton felt a ghastly wrenching sensation inside him, as the weight of the axe's thick ice-cold iron entered his neck, severing his vocal cords: his head fell limp and dangled precariously from his shoulders, his neck spurting plumes of blood; after a second blow it tumbled extravagantly along the ground. After several rolls its momentum finally ceased, and the headsman bounded forward to collect it and held it up proudly – like some kind of shining trophy – for all to see, and placed it, almost lovingly, into a bucket-like vessel at his side. Half the crowd cheered emotively, yelling *'traitor!'* Cromwell smiled sinisterly out of view. A few ravens bounced happily on the Tower's stone, as Smeaton's headless body was dragged from the Block: a thick trail of blood marking his path from his still convulsing heart.

Next up was the venerable Henry Norris – the man who had requested to duel with the King in defense of Anne's honour. His final words were: 'I would rather die a thousand deaths than be guilty of *such* a falsehood.'

George Boleyn said a far longer and more personal farewell.

You all, and especially you my masters of the Court, that you will trust in God, and not on the vanities of the world, for if I had so done, I think I had been alive as you be now; also I desire you to help to the setting forth of the true word of God; and whereas I am slandered by it, I have been diligent to read it and set it forth truly; but if I had been as diligent to observe it, and done and lived thereafter, as I was to read it and set it forth, I had not come here to, wherefore I beseech you all to be worker and live thereafter, and not to read it and live not thereafter. As for my offences, it cannot prevail you to hear them that I die here for, but I beseech God that I may be an example to you all, and that all you may be made aware by me, and heartily I require you all pray for me, and to forgive me if I have offended you, and I forgive you all, and God save the King.

Sir William Brereton said, 'The cause whereof I die judge not. But if thou judge, judge thee best.'

And lastly, Sir Francis Weston's final words were: 'I had thought to have lived in abomination yet these twenty or thirty years, and then to have made amends.'

Barrels of water were tipped to wash away the thick pools of blood that the ravens had started feeding on; and the dead were buried, along with their heads, within the Tower. Everyone that had come to witness the bloody spectacle had not cheered when the heads of the others were raised by the headsman. It wasn't as if they weren't used to seeing these sorts of gruesome acts carried out, and were horror-struck by it. It was the fact that almost all the condemned men had not confessed their guilt, which was not a good sign that the trials were carried out justly. The public's suspicion seemed validated, and anger for their King was once again at boiling point. The Tower's officials did not want a similar reaction during Anne Boleyn's execution; so they rearranged it to take place later in the week, and at a different time of day.

Anne tried to set her mind on things less gloomy as the fateful day neared. Peering through her chamber window, she watched the occasional bird fly freely through the air, and gazed at the full moon as it lit up a dense dark night. She wrote poetry, and sang as she played her lute; and for fleeting seconds, it must have felt, Anne infused the air with playful waves of music that traveled far into the lonely depths of the fortress, where surely her brother had been kept.

Poem by Anne Boleyn

Defiled is my name full sore,
Through cruel spite and false report,
That I may say for evermore,
Farwell, my joy! Adieu comfort!
For wrongfully ye judge of me,
Unto my fame a mortal wound,
Say what ye list, it will not be,
Ye seek for that can not be found

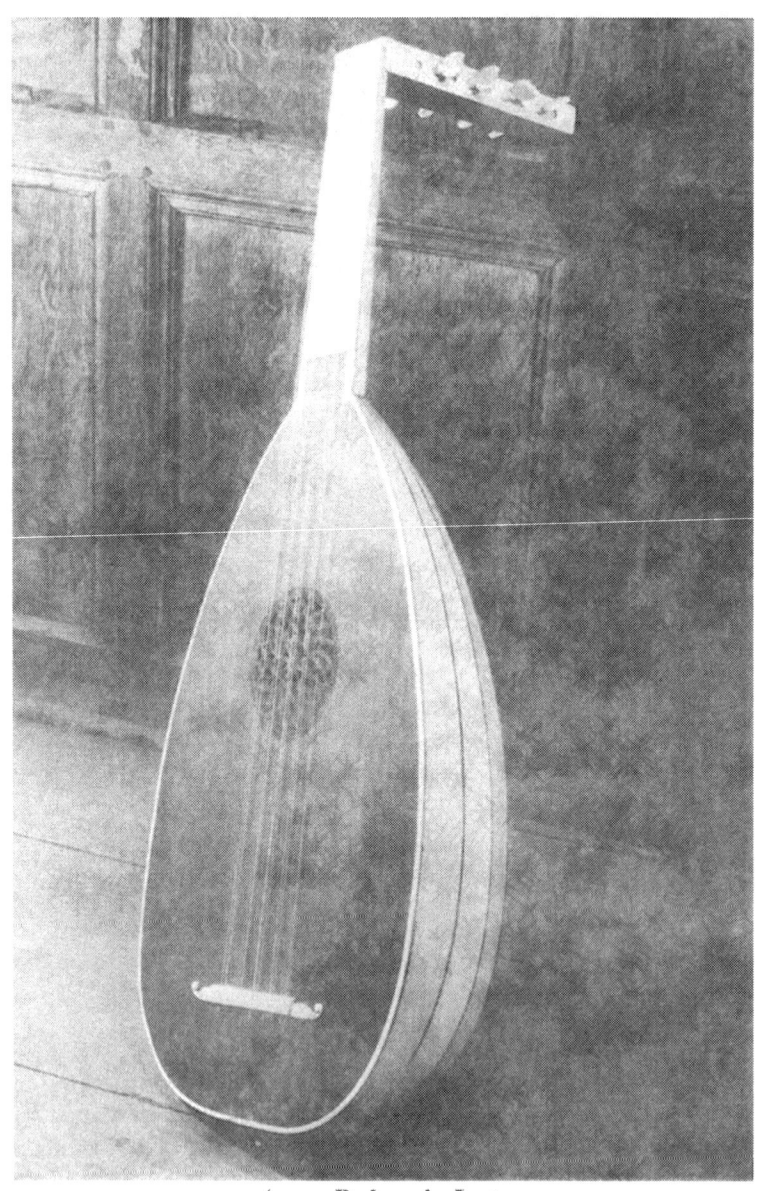

Anne Boleyn's Lute

FINAL DAYS

On May 16th, 1536 the Archbidhop of Canterbury arrived at the Tower to provide Anne with Absolution, and one other thing. His visit was in part arranged by Henry to have his marriage to Anne Boleyn annuled. He discussed with Anne what the King had asked of him, and a glimmer of hope glittered in her deep brown eyes: the King sought to annul their marriage, which would mean her sentence *might* not be carried out.

That evening Anne had dinner with the Tower's constable. She told him all about her meeting with the Archbishop, and the prospect she might be set free, if the Archbishop could prove her case. Kingston remained quiet throughout the dinner, feeling it not his place to weigh in on the sensitive subject; but listening all the while with open-ears and an amiable countenance, as Anne spoke like someone who had just been given a new lease on life.

Kingston had enjoyed Anne Boleyn's company, ever since he had first met her at her coronation. But he beared the scars of his profession, and years within the Tower had taught him not to become attached to anyone outside its walls: so often they met their end *here*.

With time running thin, Cranmer dispatched a letter to Henry, and another to Anne, asking them both to appear at his Ecclesiastical Court at Lambeth, to show some reason why the annulment should not be passed.

Next day the Archbishop arrived a little late for the hearing, as his fellows sat waiting, ready to pass the annulment. In Henry's mind, Anne was finished; and he wasn't about to give her a chance to haunt his memory right before she died. He wanted her nowhere near him now, so he appointed Dr. Sampson and Drs. Wotton to appear on their behalf.
The Earl of Oxford and the Duke of Suffolk, as well as other members of the Court listened as Cranmer declared his judgment on the marriage, before providing them with the statement Anne gave him the day before. The Court considered his judgement before giving theirs, and they also agreed that the marriage should be annuled. But, crucially, they concluded that Anne and Henry had been legally married; so her punishment remained unchanged. It was sealed. Anne would be beheaded on the Tower green on May 19th, 1536 at eight o'clock in the morning.

*

With one day to go preparations had taken place and everything was ready. A small scaffold had been built, and the famous headsman from Calais, Jean Rombaud, had arrived on time; he was commisioned by the

King because Anne had requested for a skilled headsman, and to die by the sword rather than the axe.

Darkness descended upon the Tower, and the marching died down as the guards conducted their last exhibition drill. Later that night Anne called for the almoner to provide her with solace. The lone guard shifted once every hour; each change echoed loudly as their hard-heeled boots tapped ruthlessly aginst the Tower's stone, like the inexorable ticking of a clock.

With the hours closing in, thoughts of those final moments went flooding through her mind –

* * *

Morning dawned, and the grey dismal day unveiled itself. Anne dressed in a loose dark-grey gown of damask and a white coif and black headdress. Not surprisingly, she hadn't slept the night before, having been apprehensive of the frightening day ahead of her and determined to live every last precious second of her life until she would have it no more.

Anne asked an attendant to deliver a letter she had written to Kingston; it was a request for him to be with her in such time that she would receive the good Lord. Kingston respectfully heeded to her wish. The time of Anne's execution had been changed that morning, as further attempt to catch the public off-guard.

When Kingston arrived at Anne's chamber she said, 'I hear I shall not die before noon, and I am very sorry therefore, for I thought I would be dead by this time and past my pain.'

'There will be little pain,' he said softly.

Anne knew Kingston well enough by now that his long periods of silence did not unsettle her; and during those final days in the Tower she found it easy to be herself in his presence. 'I heard say the executioner was very good, and I have a *little* neck,' she said, putting her hands to it and laughing heartily. A small smile could just be discerned on Kingston's deeply lined face.

Anne made her final preparations; and after setting her eyes upon her reflection for one last time, at eleven o'clock she followed Kingston through the halls, accompanied by no less than one hundred Yeoman Warders. As they passed the corridor windows, Anne glanced out at the grounds below; three thousand or more crowded men and women stood there.

Once out in the cool dewy air, the ash-grey sky above seemed to aggrandize her very presence. A light misty rain was falling through the fog; the sensation of icy water carresing her awoke her soul. The odd raven flew blackly under the darkening sky, or perched high on the wall's edge, surveying the mass that had gathered below. For how many people were within the Tower's walls, the mood remained sombre; under it all, however, the public was yearning to see their captivating Queen for one last time.

Anne was led to the green, next to the White Tower. At once the crowd fell silent, as everyone turned magnetically towards her. She walked towards the four-foot high scaffold, which had been designed to minimize her exposure to the crowd, and, alone, stepped up on to the platform where the headsman stood. Looking like he hadn't a care in the world, as Anne Boleyn approached him he found himself dumbfounded, and for a few seconds had completely forgotten why he was standing there, in front of so many people.

She observed the executioner impassively, which seemed to bring him back to reality, before turning her eyes to the crowd, looking for familiar faces in the bundle of heads standing motionless before her. Almost all of the King's Council was there, as well as numerous earls, lords, alderman, merchants, sheriffs, accomplised businessmen, and artists. Anne's father wasn't there; perhaps he felt guilty for having ever made ties with the King, and was overcome with grief. Her uncle, the Duke, failed to show up; Anne felt relieved that his merciless eyes would not be one of the last things she gazed into. The Duke of Suffolk, who knew her personally, was present, and stood by the other nobles. Thomas Cromwell had, not suprisingly, come to watch the *finale* of his master plan; he lingered amongst the rest, trying hard not to catch Anne's eye. The Lord Mayor of London, who
felt strongly that the trials were of the King's design, stood high among his fellows, beaming consolingly at Anne as she gazed admiringly back.

The mist slowly began to transform into a gentle rain, becoming heavier and heavier with each solid second that passed. The sky darkened; everything became still and shadowy; rain falling hard against the tower's stone, producing a steady *rush* and rythmic *rattle* as if the sky itself had decided to perform a drum roll. The headsman's sword lay hidden from view; its presence no longer disguised as rain sounded off of of the long blade. Anne said good-bye.

ANNE BOLEYN'S GHOST

Masters, I here humbly submit me to the law as the law hath judged me, as for my offences, I here accuse no man, God knoweth them; I remit them to God, beseeching him to have mercy on my soul, and I beseech Jesu save my soveriegn and master the King, the most godly, noble and gentle Prince that is, and long to reign over you.

She removed her head dress, knelt down on both knees, looked up to the tearful sky and closed her eyes; water falling like heavan's breath upon her.

... Jesu Christ I commend my soul ...

The headsman lifted the sword from behind the straw; water ran from the blade in a small torrent. The movements of the sword seemed to resonate an unseen energy that Anne could feel distinctly, though her eyes were closed, as the headsman swung it to and fro in preparation. An ominous drone issued from it.

Raising the sword with both arms, he swung and beheaded her with as much ease, she felt no greater than a rose. Her headless body fell, blooming a river of blood under the stormy sky. Her lips trembled ... her eyes faded ... her face turned white as snow.

She was being carried on a wave, completely at its mercy. She was dead ... she *was* dead – but she could see dark transient *forms* of men and women standing in front of her. They began to move away from her; they were leaving.

Cannon fire boomed and iron tore through the air over London, signaling to the King that it was over. The crowd poured out of the Tower, making for the nearest pubs to get dry. The Tower's officials had failed to prepare a suitable coffin for Anne Boleyn. Her body was disgracefully placed, curled up and on its side, into an empty arrow-chest they had managed to find. Her 'coffin' was then taken to the Tower's Chapel of St. Peter ad Vincula, and buried within. It remains there to this day.

Sightings of Anne's Ghost

Anne Boleyn's Ghost is one of the most frequently seen ghosts in England. Below are just some of the numerous accounts that have taken place over the centuries of sightings of her Ghost. At times she has been witnessed by many; but, as is common with ghost sightings, it is almost always by the lone individual. Some of the accounts here have varying degrees of credibility, while others are much harder to dispute.

At the Tower of London, in the chapel where Anne Boleyn was buried, there are accounts of her Ghost carrying her head under her arm whilst walking down the aisle and descending into her grave. Other areas of the Tower where Anne's Ghost has been reported by members of the public and the Tower's staff over the years are the Green, the White Tower, and the room she stayed in before her coronation and execution.

In 1864, a sentry standing outside the 'Queens House' reported seeing a misty white figure of a woman wearing a Tudor dress and a French hood. When he looked at the woman's face, he saw nothing there. As the apparition started to move towards him, he demanded to know who she was. The sentry then yelled at the headless woman, who had been steadily approaching him, to stop; and when she failed to comply he charged at her with his bayonet and passed clean through her misty form.

At that exact same moment a burst of electricity moved along his rifle and up his arm, shocking him and knocking him out. He later found himself court martialed for falling asleep on duty. At his trial he described what he had seen.

'It was a figure of a woman wearing a queer looking bonnet, but there wasn't no head inside the bonnet.' When eyewitnesses came to his defense, saying that they had also seen a headless woman that night; and a guard from inside the *Bloody Tower* recalled the whole bizzare encounter, which he saw unfold from a second story window, the charges were immediately dropped.

Towards the end of the nineteenth century, on a quiet night inside the Tower, a captain of the Guard witnessed a strong fiery light coming from inside the Chapel of St. Peter ad Vincula. He tried to enter, but the door was locked. When he returned with a ladder and peered through a window, so as to see who was inside, he claimed to have seen something very peculiar indeed.

'Slowely down the aisle moved a statley procession of Knights and Ladies, attired in ancient costumes; and in front walked an elegant female whose face was averted to him, but whose figure greatly resembled the one in reputed portraits of Anne Boleyn. After having repeatedly paced the chapel, the entire procession, together with the light, dissapeared.' (excerpt from Ghostly Visitors by 'Spectre Stricken', London 1882.)

At Blickling Hall in Norfolk, on the day when Anne was executed, every year a carriage being pulled by six headless horses and a headless coachman can be seen approaching the Hall. A woman, who sits inside the carriage dressed in white, holds her head in her lap. Once there, the horses and coach disappear; and the headless woman, who then enters the Hall, wanders there until sunrise.

At Marwell Hall, legend holds that this was the place where Henry stayed with Jane Seymore during Anne's execution. It is said that a chain of beacons were lit to signal the death of Anne Boleyn – with the last beacon being near here and in clear view from the Hall.
Anne's Ghost has been seen on the yew tree walk.

At Windsor Castle, Anne's Ghost has been seen standing at a window in Dean's Cloister. The ghosts of Henry the Eighth and Elizabeth the First have been seen here on separate occasions. The castle is a hub of paranormal phenomena, and countless ghosts of historical figures have been witnessed here. The Ghost of Elizabeth the First is the most frequently seen ghost in the castle, and has been witnessed in the Royal Library on several occasions.

At Anne Boleyn's lifelong home, Hever Castle, her Ghost can be seen every Christmas Eve crossing the old drawbridge. Her Ghost has also been seen beneath the great oak tree, where Henry may have asked her to marry him.

At Hampton Court, Anne's Ghost has been seen wearing a blue dress. Could it be the same dress she's wearing in the photograph, which was taken at Hever Castle? The account of the sighting here was described as a sombre and slow moving apparition.